Damaged but Powerful

Steve Higgs

To my wife, Gemma, and the unborn daughter inside her. Both of whom have put up with my endless novelist prattling for long enough.

Contents

Prologue: The Sword of God

T he rain hitting my eyelashes made them twitch but I refused to let them close, or wipe my face. They had me cornered this time and without Daniel to help me escape through a portal, I had no choice but to face them down. That Daniel ran away at the last moment shouldn't have surprised me, but it did. I knew he was traumatised by all that happened to him, but he *is* a demon for goodness sake, he ought to be a little tougher than this.

The remaining three horsemen spread themselves out, trying to divide my attention as they closed in. When I killed their colleague a week ago in Egypt, I don't think they could believe it. They are the four horsemen, quite literally of the apocalypse, and one of them got ended forever by a twenty-three-year-old, five-foot one-inch woman with a missing left hand. Sure, they had seen me dispatch others of their race, but immortality had made them complacent.

Not any more though. Not since Egypt.

From the centre of my body, I pulled source energy, the primal juice that makes the Earth spin. It fuelled my ability to produce a weapon that startled me the first time I used it. With God's sword held in my prosthetic left hand, I pushed the energy from my core, feeling the familiar crackling, fizzing sensation as it moved out through my chest to my right shoulder and down to my right hand where it formed an orb that hovered just a fraction of an inch above the skin. It was a warning to them; this was sinfire they could see, the angels' magical soul essence used as a weapon. It was an abomination to the angels, though they used it in the same way themselves when they had to. Though it was potent, it was nothing compared to the hellfire the demons would produce. Were it not for my almost unique ability to create a lasting beam of it that powered the God sword, my threat to the horsemen might be minimal - I am tough, but I'm not immortal, and they are.

I checked over my right shoulder. Feeling like a batsman about to steal a base, I had to check their relative positions and judge which of them was going to try to move first.

It was the one to my right! He fired twin orbs of dark, burning red hellfire, the demons' primary weapon and one which would kill most creatures the moment it touched them, humans included. Not me though, I was somehow able to absorb it, spindle it and use it against them and they knew that, so why did he use it when he knows how ineffectual it is?

As a distraction, of course. His friends moved in the moment my attention was drawn. All three were now converging on me, the two who hadn't fired pulling longswords from their backs. As danger threatened, the pieces of God's armour I'd been able to collect so far came to life above my skin. It was less than a third of the full suit, but the parts of me they covered would be safe from harm.

The horsemen came at me from three directions; their intention to pin me in the middle where I would find it impossible to defend myself. That is why I picked the one wielding hellfire and ran at him. With my teeth gritted and a scream of rage escaping my contorted lips, I switched hands, bringing the God sword into my right where I pushed a stream of sinfire into it. The impossibly sharp obsidian blade came to life as light blue energy lit it from the inside. I had seen demons attempt to wield the sword in this way but none of them had been able to. There was only one other I had met who I felt certain could do so and he wasn't actually a demon per se. Then there was another, his brother, who I suspected likely capable of doing so. He was a demon, their leader in fact, and the world would be in deep shit if he ever got hold of it.

Which was precisely what the horsemen were here to arrange.

As the sword reached full power, I leapt and swung. The horseman swerved the blow but hadn't expected that I would fold my legs and land on my knees. My forward momentum carried me beneath his own sword as he brought it from his back in a sweeping arc and my arm slashed at his lower legs, tagging his left shin to open a deep cut that felled him.

Still sliding on my knees, I used my left hand to grab the ground and spin myself, coming up into a crouch as the other two horsemen arrived next to their colleague. I risked a smile in their direction, my chestnut hair falling across my face to hide the scar until I flicked it out of the way. 'Feeling nervous, boys?'

In reply to my question, the fallen horseman got back up, his wound refusing to heal because the God Sword made it. This was likely the first time he had bled in over four thousand years. It was the most annoying thing about the demons: their immortality. No matter what I did, they came back unharmed. Until I got my hands on the sword that is.

Even so, they were desperately hard to kill. But not impossible, as I proved in Egypt. I need to back up a bit though. I just realised I got way ahead of myself and brought you in kinda halfway through. I bet none of this even makes sense to you at this point. Let me back up a bit and start again.

It was a hot day in the United Republic of Zannaria ...

Chapter 1

Five months before the fight with the horsemen

I tipped my head back and drank the water. It was so hot it was foul, but it was all I had. It was June and the heat of the early summer in the desert made everything hot, the water was the worst, though; it was like drinking from a freshly drawn bath. Everyone in the platoon faced the same issue and each of us kept quiet about it: no one likes a whinger.

'Are we going in, boss?' The voice came from just behind me, Sergeant Baker wanting to know what we were going to do. Ahead of us was a village. We had a great view of it because we had approached from the hills to the west and were looking down over it now. It might have been standing on this spot for a century or ten centuries but who knew how much longer it would stand in the current political climate.

Zannaria was in utter turmoil again, the government collapsing under yet another coup and we were here as a peacekeeping force for the United Nations. I wore their light blue beret, though I wasn't sure how I felt about it and the very limited rules of engagement.

Atrocities were happening, vague reports circling about massacres in villages here and there as the country did its best to tear itself apart. I deployed with my platoon yesterday evening: move into position above this grid and observe. Report what you see because intel suggests this village is vulnerable.

Intel wasn't wrong; I could see the military forces parked in the village. Nothing was happening yet, but that didn't mean it wouldn't. I'm Lieutenant Anastasia Aaronson.

I joined the British Army a little more than four years ago and will get my captaincy when I return from this tour unless I manage to screw it up. Again. I am literally the longest serving Lieutenant in the British Army, held back as all my peers advanced because I cannot keep my mouth shut and have a worrying habit of telling my superiors that they are being stupid just because they are. Apparently, that's not the right thing to do.

My attitude is not a new thing and probably comes from being so small. I stopped growing at fifteen but was the smallest kid in the school on the day I started, my thumb in my mouth and a plush bunny toy tucked under my arm. A mean boy called Gavin Garson laughed and snatched my bunny that first day and a bunch of other kids laughed too. I hit him in the face with my tiny fist and took my bunny back while he held his bleeding nose. Everyone stopped laughing and backed away; that was the day I learned about how to be powerful. Now just turned twenty-three, I am five feet and one inch tall, have tiny hips and small breasts and weigh one hundred and eight pounds. It's a massive disadvantage in this environment where my gear weighs almost as much as me. I'm the one in charge though, so the fatigue and discomfort I feel can never find their way to the surface.

My attitude gained me the respect of my troops, but not that of my superiors. Well, screw them. I go to sleep every night secure in the knowledge that I did what I thought was right. Today was yet another example of the planet testing me. The absolute right thing to do, was take the heavily armed and well-trained platoon of infantry soldiers into the village below us and make sure no one did anything they shouldn't. However, I was under orders not to.

I had to observe and report. Just behind me, Sergeant Baker still waited for an answer. 'Not yet,' I replied without turning around. 'Get Corporal Travis up here. I need comms.'

This high up, with rocky terrain all around us, comms were tough and I wouldn't be able to reach anyone with the low power set I carried. I needed Corporal Travis' gear if I wanted to challenge my orders.

Waiting for him to arrive, I already knew I was going to get myself into trouble. The troops in my platoon would follow my orders without question, that much I was sure of. The question was whether I would end up facing a court-martial this time.

'Ma'am.' Corporal Travis arrived, Sergeant Baker with him as he waited for me to make a decision. The men were bored from the inactivity. Basically, they joined the armed forces to shoot shit and blow shit up and here we weren't allowed to do either. We could defend ourselves if attacked but that was about it. It didn't sit well with me or with any of them.

Corporal Travis handed me the radio handset. 'Zero-alpha this is two-four-bravo over.' I waited for an answer, then tried again when I got none. 'Zero-alpha this is two-four-bravo over.'

The radio crackled. 'Zero-alpha.'

I got an answer, that was something. 'We are in position and can see aggressive forces within the civilian population. Requesting permission to advance and secure the location against attack.' They taught us brevity as a key to secure radio transmission: get the message across but do it with as few words as possible. Well, I had done that. They knew exactly what I wanted to do and why I should do it.

There was silence from the other end as the radioman relayed my request to the colonel. Lieutenant Colonel Richard Whiting-Madesure was a politician hiding inside the uniform of a senior army officer. I spent most of my time in his presence trying to quell the desire to kick him in the bollocks. He was my commanding officer and I was one of his most junior officers. Despite that, I was utterly certain he was a tiny fraction of the man he needed to be and despite not having male genitalia, my balls were still bigger than his.

The silence on the radio stretched out for half a minute. Then the radio crackled, and the radioman's voice returned. 'Negative two-four-bravo, remain in an observation pattern.'

I opened my mouth to voice my thoughts on the matter, but a shot echoed across the valley, emanating from the village and telling me that the brewing trouble down there had just bubbled over.

I still had the handset in my hand. 'Zero-alpha, shots fired. Shots fired. We are advancing to secure the civilian population.' I was already pulling my primary weapon into my shoulder and thinking about which line of approach would provide my troops with the best shelter.

The response from zero alpha came back less than a second later. 'Negative two-four-bravo. You are not to engage. Observe and report only.'

I took a breath, pushing down my rising anger as I snarled into the radio again. 'Put him on the radio.'

There was a moment of silence before the voice at the other end changed. 'Two-four-bravo I am not used to being barked at. You had better make this good.'

I did my best to still my rage as I spoke, 'There is a civilian population in danger. I am going to protect them.'

'No, you are not, two-four-bravo. That is not your mission.'

'To hell with my mission and to hell with you. Do you really think I should sit here while the villagers are tortured or killed? There are children in that village. I can see them from here.'

'I understand your concern, but that doesn't change the fact that we are here on a peacekeeping mission...'

I cut him off. 'Good. I'm off to keep the peace. Out.' I let the radio send switch go and pulled my rifle into my shoulder, feeling the weight of it and taking comfort from its solidity. This whole situation pissed me off. I joined the army to make a difference, to be someone, to stand up for those who couldn't stand up for themselves. Now, here I was facing exactly that situation, and they expected me to do nothing.

Over my shoulder, I growled. 'Sergeant Baker, get them ready. We move in two.'

'What are we going to do, boss?'

'Nothing,' I assured him. 'We are going to walk into that village and look dangerous because if we do that right, we won't have to do anything. We can stop them from doing things that will haunt them, and us, just by being there.' I knew I was right. We wouldn't need to fire a shot. I could disobey my orders and yet obey them too. I was to observe, but I could do that better if I was a lot closer. I wouldn't break any of the rules of engagement,

I wouldn't endanger my troops, but I would stop a massacre from happening if that was what the soldiers in that village had in their heads.

We had been hunkered down in the rocks and invisible to anyone that cared to look our way since we arrived under cover of darkness, but I stood up now, silhouetting myself as I came over the rocks to start my way down toward the village. Our clothing was camouflaged to vanish into the scenery if we stayed still, but thirty-seven advancing blue berets were going to be hard to miss.

A flutter of nerves unsettled my stomach, but I bit them down too. There was a job to do and no one had put me here except me. Behind me was an infantry platoon of soldiers, all looking for me to guide them. Many of them had wives and children at home and wanted to return to them in one piece. Part of my job was to make sure that happened. Even so, there was a job to do and we had to place ourselves in harm's way to do it.

Hand commands and gestures spread the platoon out as we crossed the open ground. I felt my senses were on high alert and imagined the rest of the troops felt the same. My eyes were taking in everything ahead of me, my synapses on overload, waiting for someone to take a shot at us.

Nothing happened though. We came down out of the rocks, a mass of heavily armed soldiers and easy to spot because of the stupid light blue berets. There was no way the troops in the village hadn't seen us. We got down to the valley floor unopposed, though, which was good. If they opened fire to scare us off, I would face a tough decision about what to do next. The ideal situation was for us to walk into the village and for the Zannarian rebel soldiers to leave. But at this stage, I couldn't even be sure which faction they were from. Doing this was the sort of manoeuvre that won a person a medal. Not that a medal even came into my thoughts; I couldn't care less about such things. I just wanted to be able to sleep at night.

What happened next was my fault though. You can call it a lack of forethought, or poor judgement or maybe just bad luck, but I hadn't considered the terrain between us and the village. I hadn't given it the slightest thought.

Sergeant Baker knew when he stepped on a landmine. I saw him react in that split second between the click and the detonation. He glanced my way and then he was gone, his expression of disbelief forever and indelibly etched into my brain. I had but a moment to register it before pieces of shrapnel hit me and everything went black.

Chapter 2

Four months later, I was meeting my new flatmate.

When the blast from the landmine hit me, I lost my left foot just below the ankle and my left hand just above the wrist. As injuries go, they were fairly awful, but I had prosthetics to replace them. It was the piece of shrapnel that hit my left cheek which did the real damage. It is still inside my brain where sooner or later it will kill me. It ruined the left side of my face, not that I ever fooled myself that I was pretty, but my blue eyes and flowing chestnut hair gave me a certain something, I thought. They shaved one half of my skull so the chestnut hair, even four months on, wasn't long enough to hide the scar on my left cheek, but even the ruined face wasn't the real damage. No, it gets worse yet. The tiny piece of shrapnel sliced through my amygdala and tore out my memory.

I hadn't lost the ability to do anything, I knew how to speak and work the tv remote, how to switch on the lamp and I could probably still strip and reassemble my weapon without needing a manual, albeit the task would now have to be done one-handed. However, personal memories, my childhood, my first pet, or whether I even had one, joining the army; all these things were gone and were unlikely to ever come back the doctors assured me. My mother and sister came to see me in the hospital, both crying and wanting to hug me, though, so far as my brain was concerned, I had never seen either before in my life. New memories were forming and staying, the doctors telling me how lucky I was that the damage wasn't worse. I didn't feel lucky.

Unsurprisingly, my army career was over. I could have hung around and found a rear-echelon job, could have dragged out my discharge for a few years for sure, but I couldn't be what I wanted to be, so I wasn't going to remain in that environment and torture myself. Technically I am still in the army, they are still paying me at least, but I signed all the paperwork before I left the hospital, and my official discharge date would catch up with me soon enough.

I found a job via the armed forces resettlement services. It was in a library in Rochester. I had only a vague idea where Rochester was so had to look it up on a map and then read about it, but it ticked enough boxes for me to apply for the position, have a phone interview and agree to start the following week. All I had to do then was find a place to stay, which proved easy enough via a room-to-let website, and I could arrange for the army to deliver my things to the address I then had.

I didn't own much, some clothes, a few DVDs and electronic devices, sports gear and a semi-decent laptop. That was about it and it all came in one large cardboard box which I myself had filled before I went to Zannaria. It was standard army practice to have soldiers pack up their rooms before they went away. It made it a lot easier to deal with if they didn't return, which, inevitably, someone always didn't.

My new flatmate was a young woman called Sarah Bishop. Needing a place to stay, I had agreed to the room rate in her small flat and figured I could put up with it for six months (the minimum contract term) no matter how bad it was. It wasn't bad though, which is to say I had endured far worse. The rent was cheap, I was only renting a bedroom after all, and it was about all I could afford because the job at the library didn't exactly pay a lot. It was something to get me started and that was all I needed. The rooms were small and the flat itself was small. The kitchen had just about enough room for both of us to stand in, but a third person would need lubricant to join us it was that much of a squeeze. The décor was drab but tidy and I could tell Sarah had put some effort into tidying the place before I got there.

When I arrived, late because of leaves on the line delaying the train, plus the usual slow Sunday service, she was already impatient to leave and made a big point of showing me that I had held her up. Until she bothered to look at me that is.

'Oh, wow,' she said, taking in my scarred face and my prosthetic hand. Then self-conscious, she said, 'Sorry, that was rude of me.'

'It's okay,' I told her. 'It surprises me too sometimes.' I had taken to wearing hoodies for the first time in my life, the hood doing the job of hiding my face, so people didn't see the scar and stare. No one had looked my way on the train, not that I could see them tucked deep inside the material. Nor could I hear them with my ear buds in and Axl Rose proving his lyrical brilliance once again.

Sarah shook her head and welcomed me off the doormat and into her flat. It was a small two-bedroom place located close to the river in what I soon learned was the marina end of Rochester. Leading me through to her kitchen, she started apologising again. 'When you said you were injured, I guess I didn't really think about what that might mean.'

'It's my fault,' I assured her. 'I should have been more specific.' I had a heavy bag over my right shoulder which I slid off awkwardly and dumped on the floor. I was still getting used to the new arm and not using it much for fear it would just fall off or I would drop whatever I was holding.

'Is it ... is it just what I can see? Sorry,' she apologised yet again. 'I mean ... you don't have to tell me anything. I guess ... I guess I'm just curious.'

I had explained my injuries several dozen times now and knew I would be doing so again in the coming week as I met lots of new people. I held up my carbon fibre robotic left hand so she could see it, and said, 'I lost my left foot as well so now I have a plastic one. I won't be taking up ballet any time soon.' My throwaway comment made her chuckle which was the effect I wanted to escape the chance of sympathy. Sympathy would get me nowhere and start a spiral that would lead to everyone feeling sorry for the poor crippled girl with the ruined face.

Sarah kept glancing at the clock on the oven, clearly anxious to leave but feeling it would be impolite to do so, so soon after I arrived.

'Do you have a date?' I asked, not wanting to hold her up.

She laughed at the concept; a fake laugh that was supposed to be perceived as such. 'I wish. No nothing like that. There's an England football game and I am supposed to be meeting some friends to watch it.'

'Don't let me hold you up. I wouldn't want you to miss it.' She wasn't dressed in a football strip or wearing anything that might suggest she was going out to support a team. In fact, her outfit screamed *I'm on a date*, though I didn't mention it.

'Is that okay?' she asked. It was clear she really wanted to get going, her feet were already moving toward the door. Then she stopped and turned to me with an expression that said she'd just had an idea. 'You should come with me. There will be lots of people there. Oh,' she glanced down at my left foot. 'It's about a mile to walk.'

Like my injuries, I could see I was going to find myself explaining my limitations, or lack thereof, many times. 'Walking is no problem. I can run even.' I had practiced on the treadmill at the hospital, finding the hardest part wasn't the lack of sensation in my left foot, but the weight imbalance caused by my fake arm. 'That's okay though, I don't think I'm ready to be out in public yet.'

She bit her lip, wondering if she should encourage me or not, then accepted my answer and picked up her handbag from the kitchen counter. 'Two removal men turned up with a box of your stuff yesterday. I had them put it in your room. I hope that's okay. Help yourself to whatever you find in the fridge, there's takeaway menus on the pin board but you probably just use an app like everyone else. I'll not be late back; I have work tomorrow.' I got a quick wave as she left the kitchen but as she opened the door, I kicked myself and went after her.

'I've changed my mind. Is that okay?' The truth was that I really didn't want to go out. However, I hadn't had a drink in almost a year with the operational tour in Zannaria and then my recuperation in hospital. Right now, I really wanted one. Meeting people and being in public places where everyone would stare at my face was something I could do without but I also knew I had to accept my new reality, so, like everything else that ever scared me, I ran at it headfirst. I wasn't really dressed for going anywhere. The bulk of my civilian clothes were still in my box so what I had was what I took to Zannaria with me for the rare occasion when we rotated off the front and into a base. My black leggings and running shoes had seen better days and the light-grey hoody was one I was given in hospital and two sizes too big for me. It had the name of a thrash metal band on the front and tour dates on the back, but it wasn't like I was going to be out trying to pick up men, so it didn't matter what I looked like.

On the way there, a good mile and half walk, I learned all about Sarah. She was happy to chat about herself but showed little interest in asking the same questions of me; something I encouraged by asking her more questions. Sarah was twenty-seven and grew up in the area. She almost married but caught him cheating on her and hadn't spoken to him since. She said it was a real shame because she liked his mum better than her own. She had a job as the receptionist in a dentist surgery in Rochester High Street and had worked there since she left school at sixteen. Over the course of twenty minutes, because she walked slowly, that was about all I learned, other than she was unhappy about her body because it was a bit pudgy in places, her words not mine, and she really ought to do some exercise in her opinion. The only other snippet of detail she let slip was that she hated football and her sole reason for going tonight was a boy called Ian who she hoped to snare. It explained her outfit at least.

She was pleasant enough and I figured we could be friendly if not friends. We had little in common though; like most people, I found her to be very self-centred – all the decisions in her life were about how she could do better for herself, no thought spared for others. I didn't comment on it and spent most of my time nodding along and taking in the wonderful skyline as we approached the ancient castle sitting on the banks of the river near the bridge. Reaching that, she took a right turn to lead me up a steep incline and into the castle grounds where we emerged into an open space dominated by a cathedral. The late summer sun hung behind it, making the roof seem to glow and there were countless people, tourists probably, moving about in front of its doors.

Just beyond that was an old stone gate, like the fortified entrance to an ancient walled city, and beyond that was the vibrant High Street, teeming with life and beckoning to everyone but a girl with a face she wanted no one to see.

Sarah said, 'It's not far now. Just around the corner to the left. It's quite a walk, isn't it? I usually get a taxi back.'

I didn't think it was far at all but didn't say that, understanding that my perception of what was far, or tough, or difficult was skewed by testing my absolute limits in the army.

The bar really was just around the corner though, a place called Eddy's Tavern. Sarah led me in through one of a pair of swing doors to the packed public house beyond. The football match was already underway, and the crowd were relatively quiet. That would change, of course, the moment someone scored, more so if it was the home team.

Sarah spotted her friends and waved to get their attention. I tapped her elbow. 'I'll get drinks. What would you like?'

Without even turning her head my way, she said, 'A white wine spritzer.' Then she was gone, and I got to see her loop her arm through a man's elbow as she reached the group, getting tactile instantly though it was clear from his body language that the man had no interest in her.

At the bar, a tall, thin man with an impressive beard and a waxed mustache that curled up at the ends, turned his attention my way. I pointed to one of the pumps. 'A pint of pale ale please and a white wine spritzer.'

He didn't move to get a glass as one might expect, but said, 'Sorry, I need to ask your age, or see your face. Most people take their hoods off when they come in. Do you have some ID, please?' My face was down because I didn't want to look at people. I didn't want to see them staring at the left side of my face, but I hadn't thought my policy through so here I was, trying to get my first alcohol in months and already failing.

I looked up at him and reached into my back pocket where I had a bill fold and my driving licence. Just as I pulled it out, I heard a whisper, an odd little noise that seemed to come from inside my skull. I snapped my head around, expecting to find someone behind me but the space there was empty.

I turned back to find the barman examining my driver's licence and bending down to see inside my hood. 'I'll need to see your face,' he said.

I understood why. At five feet one inch tall and weighing barely more than a hundred pounds, I could be a ten-year-old boy under the hood. It wasn't as if I had an impressive chest to make the front of my hoody look feminine. Reluctantly, I reached up with both hands and pulled the hood back so he could see my face. My hair was growing in, but not

15

fast enough for me to use it to hide my scar. Across the bar I heard a gasp and saw a man nudge his girlfriend.

The barman nodded. 'Thank you, Anastasia. I'm Anton. I'm here all the time. If you come back in, just come to me. I'll make sure you get served.' Wordlessly, I put my hood back up, disappearing inside it where I felt safer as he poured my drinks.

The whispering came again. A hungry noise, somewhere deep in the back of my brain. I could hear it clearly, the words distinct and not like I was hearing it over the noise of the crowd. Once again, I turned around but could not discern where the sound was coming from.

'Feed!'

This time the voice startled me, making me jump as if touching a live wire. Much louder than the whispers, this time there was no question it arrived inside my head without bothering to go through my ears.

'Are you alright?' asked Anton, placing two drinks on the bar.

With wide eyes, I didn't know how to answer his question, so I fumbled for my money and pressed a ten into his hand. 'Keep the change,' I mumbled as I grabbed the drinks.

You might wonder how I can pick up something as delicate as a glass filled with liquid using a prosthetic hand. A few years ago it would not have been possible, but fate smiled on me, if you wish to see it that way; my age plus the nature of my injury made me a candidate for a new prosthetic developed by a firm called Real Limb. Where my left hand used to be, I now had what was basically a bionic attachment. It had been moulded and fitted to meet my exact needs, so it was the same size as my tiny right hand. It picked up electrical impulses from the muscles in my arm, translating them into movements. Controlling it accurately took a little practice, but Real Limb had videos of pianists and violinists playing their instruments with replacement hands. If they could do that, I could carry a drink.

Despite that, when Anton saw my prosthetic hand - I could have got one that was matched to the tone of my skin but I thought the white carbon fibre was cooler – he came to my rescue. 'Here,' he said, picking it up for me. 'Where are you heading?' I pointed to Sarah and the gaggle of people she was with, then started toward her around the bar as Anton crossed inside to exit via a lift-up flap.

Sarah saw me coming and looked confused for a moment until she saw Anton converging on her as well. She took the drink from him. 'Thank you, Anton.' I thanked him too and got a nod in return as he made his way back to the bar.

'This one is old and shrivelled. I want fresh and young.' Once again, the voice sounded in my head. It was making me feel dizzy.

A reply came back, and with it a sense of direction. *'There will be more here. Drain this one and then we will look for another.'*

I could feel the voices. They were outside somewhere back toward the cathedral. Hearing them was making my head spin, or was that the first sip of alcohol in months?

Next to me, Sarah placed her hand on my left shoulder. 'Everyone this is my new flat mate, Anastasia. Ana used to be a soldier, now she works at the library.' I felt like I was a prize cow being shown off at market, but I felt too dizzy to do anything to stop her.

'Where's her face?' asked one of the men. He wasn't being curious; he was being impolite.

I kept my head down, but the man next to him joked, 'Maybe she's ugly, Carl. Did you consider that? Maybe she's doing us a favour by keeping it hidden.' They were acting up because they had been drinking for a while and their comments were most likely meant in jest and not intended to be cruel. Nevertheless, I was going to leave the bar, not because of them, but because I might throw up from the nausea I now felt.

However, as the men laughed at their little joke, I pulled back my hood and shut them all up, their grins crashing to the floor like shattered glass.

I put my drink on the bar and left, shoving my way through the crowd to get to the cooler air outside. Behind me I could hear someone's girlfriend berating them for being insensitive.

Sarah caught up to me at the door. 'God, I'm so sorry, Ana. I had no idea they would be like that. They're not normally so tactless. They've been in here drinking for hours.'

'It's okay,' I told her, my head down. 'I just need some air. I'll be back soon.' Then I slipped away from her and out of the door where I could take large gulps of air and bend over to get my head low to the ground.

'We are the first here?' I heard the odd guttural voice again.

'No. There are others nearby. They have no protector here.' A second voice said.

'Not like Bremen,' the first voice agreed.

It felt like I was listening to two people argue, though the accent was odd, and their voices were more like a rasping noise - almost metallic sounding.

'Feast. Then we shall move on.'

Woozy, and using the wall to steady myself as if drunk already, I started in the direction of the voices. Whoever I was listening to, they sounded as if they were attacking someone. I worried I might be going nuts, the piece of shrapnel in my head connecting directly to a television show being aired, but curiosity, and concern, demanded I follow the noise to its source.

Clear as anything, the voices continued arguing in my head like I was listening to an audiobook recording through a set of earphones. I wouldn't be able to tell anyone why, but I could sense what direction they were in, my feet leading me back along the cobbled road toward the cathedral and then past it.

I took a left turn down an alleyway, walked across a quiet courtyard, my feet echoing in the still of the night as I left the crowds behind, then made a right turn when I reached the far side. I couldn't tell you where I was, but I appeared to be in the grounds of a school. Whatever it was, it was hundreds of years old and lit only by moonlight now that the sun had set.

This time when the voice came, I heard it with my ears because the creature speaking was standing right in front of me.

It wasn't human though and neither was his partner.

Chapter 3

There were two of them, each as butt ugly as the other. They had hairless skulls, which in the moonlight appeared to have a buttery yellow hue. They were reptilian to look at, their skin shiny like a snake or lizard and their noses were flat to their face, nothing more than two slits really and their ears were tight to their heads and slightly pointed. Otherwise they were humanoid: arms, legs, a body, and they wore human clothes.

They hadn't expected me, that was for sure, both spinning around and into defensive postures as each drew a weapon from behind their backs. They were short swords, black under the moonlight as if made from glass.

'Fresh meat,' the one on the left leered, their voices coming to me through my ears now.

Its partner sniffed the air, raising his nose like a dog might. 'It is injured.'

'Then it will be weak and easy to feed from.'

'What the hell are you?' I asked, my feet taking it upon themselves to back away.

They didn't answer. Instead, they advanced, one going left as the other went right to divide my attention. It made their shadows move which revealed a crumpled lump on the ground. It wasn't moving but I could see a hand sticking out and knew it was whatever they had been squabbling about feasting on a few moments ago.

They had attacked someone, that I was certain of, and I needed to get help for that person, but I wasn't going to have time to do that before these two ... things got to me. My brain wanted to scream for help, but for one, I had never screamed for help in my life and didn't plan to start now just because I didn't know what I was facing, and secondly, if anyone did come, the chances were they would get hurt saving me and then I would have to deal with guilt.

Better to deal with them myself. It was brave and stupid, but I was going to do it anyway. The hood was affecting my peripheral vision, so I unzipped the garment quickly and wrapped it around my prosthetic left hand. This was partly to protect it because it was shiny and new and cost a gazillion quid, but also because if they didn't see what it was maybe they would be surprised when I hit them with it since it is a lot more solid than a flesh and bone hand.

They were coming at me as if they were walking around the edge of a circle, dividing my attention but keeping me pinned in place. I switched the tables on them, pushing off with my good foot to run at the left most creature. I didn't need to be able to name what it was to be able to see that it threatened me and was going to hurt me if I didn't get my attack in first. Fortunately, one of the advantages of being tiny was that everyone always underestimated me. People didn't expect me to have learned several different martial arts disciplines and have boxed. The army loved me, or at least, the sports teams in the army had loved me. My bosses not so much, but as I closed with the creature, it looked surprised that I was attacking, glancing to its partner who had stopped moving so it could watch.

I leapt, shoving off with my right foot to lead with my prosthetic hand. I was going to club it, but the creature moved faster than I expected, its short sword swinging to parry my strike.

I had just enough time to register that it was going to cut my hand off before the blade embedded itself in the carbon fibre and stuck. Then I landed high on its chest with both knees and drove it backward. It toppled and I ripped my left arm down and away, pulling the sword from the creature's grasp. It hit the flagstones hard with me on top and I rolled with the momentum, taking the blade as my motion knocked it free. Now I was closest to their victim and I had one of their weapons.

The one who was still armed pointed its sword at me as it circled to its friend. I hadn't done any lasting damage and probably should have thought to stick the creature with the sword before I rolled away. Too late now, it was getting back to its feet.

'What are you?' the one with the sword asked. It seemed like an odd question, but I wasn't wasting any breath on conversation.

'She is not human,' observed its companion, now back on his feet and looking a little winded. 'She can see through our enchantments.'

Its companion sniffed the air again. 'She smells human.'

The second advanced, sneering, 'Let's see how she tastes then.'

That didn't sound good. They both rushed me at once, learning from their mistakes and I knew they were going to prove to be too much before they got to me. I might have learned martial arts, but who learns to fight with a sword?

Holding it awkwardly in my right hand, I tried to pick which of them I needed to swing at first. In the end, it probably wouldn't have made any difference. I swung to parry the sword as the one wielding it struck at me, but it was a deceptive tactic to get my sword arm going in one direction so the unarmed one could tackle me bodily. I saw it coming and kicked out with my solid left foot to catch it between its legs. I didn't get the effect I hoped for, the creature's anatomy different to that of a man perhaps. Hell, for all I knew they were both girls.

What did happen was it grabbed my foot and yanked it to wrench me off balance. My foot came free and it fell backward to land on its arse, the look on its face priceless. I had no time to enjoy it because its friend was still trying to stab me. I had seen movies with Robin Hood sword fighting against two, three, or even four guys at a time, yet I couldn't handle one.

Distracted by the yank to my foot, I then had to put the stump of my left leg down, which caused an eruption of pain to shoot up my leg bones. It also made me lopsided and off balance – neither thing desirable in a fight.

My sword was knocked to the side, exposing my whole body just as the one holding my foot discarded it and threw itself at me. Diving at me with its superior weight, I was driven to the ground with its arms wrapped around my torso. I tried to get the sword around to stab its head or body as I fell, but its partner stepped on my hand to pin it in place and plucked the sword from it.

'That's better,' it commented. 'Now we can feast.'

I struggled and writhed in place, bucking and kicking but they were too heavy for me to throw off. One was straddling me, keeping my hips tight to the ground as its friend held my arms. Then they both moved their heads down, one either side of me, coming for my neck like they were going to give me a hickey or something. From the corner of my eye, I saw a strange, ethereal blue light glowing from their mouths as they began to suck, and I was struck with agony. It was like they had replaced my blood with lava and my whole insides were on fire.

I couldn't imagine a worse pain, but I also felt sleepy, like my energy was being drained and the sensible thing now was to go to sleep. My eyes were heavy, wanting to close, but as they fluttered, I felt something like static electricity emanating from my chest.

The creatures stopped sucking on my neck for a moment, both lifting their heads so they could look down at me. I looked too. The static electricity was visible; dancing blue arcs of light jumping out of my skin to burrow back in again as they made their way from my chest to my right shoulder and down my arm.

'She is not human!' yelled one in terror, trying to grab for his sword.

'She must be,' argued the other, sounding equally scared, but whatever I was, I could feel power welling up from somewhere inside me and it needed to be released.

'Quick! Kill her!' yelled the one sitting on top of me, but as I screamed my defiance, its partner grabbed for my right hand and a blast of light blue energy tore from my palm to light up its face.

Its hands released my arm, flopping down as if the muscles had been switched off but as the blinding light faded, I saw why.

Its head was missing.

The remaining creature, still straddling me, lunged for a sword, but in so doing its weight came off me and I thrust upward with my hips to buck myself loose, then pulled my right hand around and fired another pulse of energy into his chest. He flew backward away from me, landing ten feet away where he started to disintegrate. Shocked by what I was seeing, I snapped my head around to look at the first creature. It was little more than dust, its clothes disintegrating as well.

My brain was doing little more than gibbering. I just shot pulses of energy from my right hand; energy that killed the two things I was fighting, and they were not human. I wasn't the type of person who believed in the unexplainable, but I couldn't explain any of what I had just witnessed. I was weak from whatever they had been doing to my neck and a sticky feeling coming from my leg stump told me I had reopened the wound there.

Then I remembered the person on the ground behind me and struggled across to them, grabbing their shoulders to check if they were alive. I felt woozy when I stood up and had to bend over again quickly to stop the world from spinning.

The victim, when I got to him, turned out to be a man, somewhere in his late forties maybe, but in poor health and living rough I was sure. He stank, but he was still breathing. His neck bore two marks, one either side where the skin was slightly puckered but neither mark was bleeding. They were roughly circular in shape and to my mind looked like a mark one might get if a vacuum cleaner was turned to high power and placed against one's skin.

With my right hand, which I couldn't stop staring at, I fished my phone out of my jeans and dialled three nines to get an ambulance. As it connected, my vision started to blur, and I had just enough warning that I was going to pass out to get my body moving in the direction of the ground before I did. Then, as a distant voice asked which service I required, my vision went black.

Chapter 4

There were stuttering sensations. The feeling of hands on me, but as I opened my eyes, all I felt was confusion. I was in an ambulance, that much I could see, but how did I get here? What terrible sequence of events befell me to bring me to this point?

I closed my eyes again and tried to remember, which was when it came flooding back to me. There were creatures in a dark courtyard. I heard them speaking from hundreds of yards away and found them as if I knew exactly where they would be. Then I fought them, and I killed them both with bolts of blue something from my right hand. Like an orb of crackling energy, I had formed it at the very centre of my being and flung it at them, blasting one's head off and firing the other ten yards across the open space. Then they both disintegrated. I was losing it. I was really losing it, my damaged brain creating hallucinations as the tiny piece of shrapnel moved and touched things inside my head that were not meant to be messed with.

A brain surgeon, whose name I could not now remember, had explained over and over that he could not predict what the shrapnel might do. It might never move. It might kill me tomorrow. I might wake up and have lost the ability to speak. If one hundred different things could happen as a consequence of my injury, ninety-nine of them were terrible and the remaining one was pretty bad.

The paramedic grabbed my right wrist and I could see her pursing her lips as she checked my pulse against the figure the monitor showed. Then she called to the driver, 'Hey, Derek, I think I'm going to have to sedate her. Her heartrate is seriously high, and her blood pressure is almost off the chart.'

From the front of the ambulance, a man's voice replied, 'Whatever you have to do. We are ten minutes out.'

I felt a sharp sting in the back of my hand and then nothing again.

The next time I opened my eyes, I was on a bed with hospital curtains drawn down both sides. Looking through my feet, I could see patients opposite and there were nurses and doctors around one of them. It looked and felt like an accident and emergency department. Trying to get a grip on myself, and forcing calm where panic wanted to rule, I tried to sit up.

That was when I discovered my right wrist was handcuffed to the bed. 'Hey!' I yelled to get attention. 'Hey!' A nurse came scurrying across, an African man in his late thirties. He had a patient expression and was utterly unbothered at seeing a small woman cuffed to the bed. Maybe he saw this most nights. 'Why am I handcuffed,' I asked, shaking my hand to rattle the cuff for emphasis.

The nurse's face was completely neutral and devoid of judgement. 'You'll have to ask the police officers that question. I will let them know you are awake.'

As he left me, I forced myself into a sitting position and tried to see if there was a clock anywhere. I couldn't see one and had no idea what time it was. Both my prosthetics were missing, and when I pulled back the covers, I discovered I had a fresh dressing on the stump of my left leg.

Mercifully, I didn't have to wait for long before someone new came along. The man who appeared around the edge of the curtain had bushy hair that was combed back but had a natural wave to it. I could smell the stench of cigarettes coming off him long before he spoke, and it explained his tired looking skin and yellowed teeth. He was a few pounds overweight, looked like he hadn't exercised in thirty years and though he looked to be closing in on sixty, I figured his real age might be the right side of fifty still. He had to be close to six feet tall and he wore thick glasses with a tortoise shell frame.

As I studied him, he produced a small fold-over ID to show me, 'I'm Detective Sergeant Spencer. I'm glad to see you are feeling better, Miss Aaronson. It is Miss Aaronson, isn't it?' He produced a notebook and looked at it, taking a pen from his pocket ready to make a new note.

'Am I under arrest?' I asked.

'Not yet,' he replied. 'It wasn't possible to read you your rights because you were unconscious and then they needed to treat you because you were bleeding and well ... not yet. How you answer my questions will determine if I have cause to arrest you or not now that you are conscious. How are you feeling?'

I ignored his question. 'If I am not under arrest, why am I cuffed to this bed?'

He raised one bushy eyebrow. 'Miss Aaronson, you were found in a dark courtyard where no person could have any decent reason to go, you were lying on top of a nearly dead homeless person who had clearly been attacked, you were unconscious but bore all the markings of a person who had been involved in a fight and there was an obsidian blade found next to you. I believe you attacked the homeless person, whose name we have yet to determine, he gave you more resistance than you expected and got in a lucky blow or something which knocked you out. Is that about right?'

My jaw was hanging open. He thought I was the aggressor. Forcing myself to be calm when I replied, I said, 'No, that is about as far from the truth as you could get. What possible reason could I have for attacking that man? I ...' what did I tell him? I couldn't say I heard the voices of the creatures who were attacking him, and it led me to find him. 'I heard a cry for help and went to investigate. There were two men attacking a third and I scared them off.' I held up my arm stump. 'Do I look like I could be out attacking people?'

He pushed out his bottom lip in a show that he acknowledged the point but wasn't entirely convinced. 'I looked you up, Miss Aaronson. You are a soldier. You still carry your military ID card, but you don't live around here. In fact, your listed base is in Shropshire. What are you doing in Rochester?'

I told the tiresome policeman about my imminent discharge, my job at the library, and gave him my new address though I had to wrack my brains to remember it. 'I arrived in

Rochester just hours before I met with the attackers, muggers, whatever they were. Is the man okay?'

'It's interesting that you should ask about him. Who is he?'

'I have no idea.' I replied frowning. 'Some poor homeless person by the look of him. Who he is doesn't matter.'

DS Spencer narrowed his eyes as he squinted at me. 'You see, I think it does matter. I think his identity is important to you and that is why you want to know if he is still alive or not.'

'What on Earth are you talking about?' I was beginning to get frustrated.

'Who is your next of kin?'

'I ... I don't have one.' Why was he asking me that? Technically, I probably still had my mother listed as my next of kin but there was no reason to contact a woman I couldn't remember.

'No next of kin,' he repeated as he made a note in his notebook. 'How is it that you have no next of kin?'

I lifted my stump to point, rather ineffectively, at my face. 'I have injuries you cannot see as well. A piece of shrapnel tore out my memory.'

He made another note. 'So, you just arrived, you don't remember anything, and you want me to believe you just stumbled upon the homeless person and scared off his attackers.'

'Yes. Can you take the cuffs off now? I really need a drink of water and I need the restroom and I can't do any of those things like this.'

He considered my question for a moment, then picked up the glass of water so he could hold it for me to drink from. I wanted to snap at him and demand he take the damned cuff off, but my throat was too sore to refuse the water. However, once I had drunk some, I tore into him. 'I'm the victim here. I'm a double amputee who went to the rescue of a person being mugged and you have me chained to a bed like a criminal. How about if I call the press?'

A smile found its way to his lips. 'Yes, that might be fun.' My threat amused him. He stopped speaking so he could look around for a chair, spotted one, and picked it up. I couldn't tell if he was being deliberately meticulous in his actions, but he took more than twenty seconds to get the chair sitting the way he wanted it. Then, once settled and looking comfortable, he said, 'Since you asked about the victim, I shall tell you that when I checked a few minutes ago, his condition was still hit and miss. When, or rather if, he regains consciousness, I shall ask for his version of events. I hope, for your sake, that he doesn't claim to have been attacked by a small woman in a hood. He has two marks on his neck that the hospital staff were not able to identify, and I notice that you have the same thing on either side of your neck. What made them, Miss Aaronson?'

I wasn't aware that they were there and moved my left hand to feel them, momentarily forgetting that I didn't have a hand there to touch my neck with. 'I don't know,' I stammered unconvincingly.

DS Spencer pursed his lips and looked at me. 'I'll tell you what, Miss Aaronson, I'm going to send a couple of uniforms to that address you gave me and see if the tenant there can corroborate your story. In the meantime, I'll get one of the hospital staff to attend to your other request.' As he got up to leave, a pair of male police officers in uniform arrived. Just beyond the curtains and out of earshot, the three men exchanged a whispered conversation. Eyes kept flicking in my direction, not that I had any doubt they were talking about me, but I raised my eyebrows in expectation when they broke their huddle, and all came toward me.

DS Spencer led. 'Miss Aaronson, the homeless person has regained consciousness. His name is David McKenzie.' He paused while checking my face to see if I reacted to the name. When I didn't, he continued. 'He was able to corroborate your story in as much as he claimed it was two men who attacked him.' He produced a key from a pocket and removed the handcuff.

Missing a hand brings all manner of basic and unexpected problems. Right now, I wanted to rub my right wrist where it had been cuffed but I couldn't use my left hand so I had to rub it on my face and on the bed, twisting and turning my arm to get to the bits of skin that were itching.

The detective sergeant wasn't finished with me yet. 'You are free to go, Miss Aaronson. I do hope I won't have cause to speak to you in the future.' As I brought my eyes up to meet his, surprised at his vaguely veiled threat, he added, 'I can tell when people are lying, Miss Aaronson. Call it policeman's intuition if you like. You lied about why you were in that courtyard. I don't know why, but be aware, please, that you are now interesting, and I shall be watching.'

Then he left, the two uniformed officers following him.

Finally alone, I drank some more water, pressed the call button to attract someone's attention because I really did need to pee and checked my phone. I had twelve missed calls from Sarah, the first a few minutes after I left the pub and the last a little after midnight in which she expressed that she hoped I hadn't got lost on my way home.

Using the voice function, I dictated a text reply. I certainly wasn't going to call her at this time, since now I had a clock to look at and could see it was quarter after one in the morning. In my message, I told her I had come across someone in need of medical attention and then been attacked myself. I was in hospital but would be out in the morning. I could have omitted the bit about getting attacked but I would then have to explain the bruises and cuts when I saw her next. This just seemed easier. Besides, she was about to have the police knock on her door.

Twenty minutes later, I was being transferred to a ward. I could have fought it, but they seemed quite concerned about my head, and they wanted to keep my left foot prosthetic off for the night to make sure the fresh wound wasn't going to be a problem. I had bruised it and split the skin. It would be sore to walk on for a while so staying the night, taking their painkillers, and trying to not fixate on the weird creatures I had fought all seemed like good ideas.

They weren't.

I should have grabbed my things and run. Possibly to another country.

Chapter 5

They kept me in for observation, concerned about the piece of shrapnel in my brain and the lump I had where my head hit the ground earlier. I didn't put up much of a fight simply because I was tired and warm and already in bed.

My sleep was restless though, dreams invading my slumber as my unconscious dragged me back to Zannaria and the face of Sergeant Baker. My memory might be screwed up, but I could see every detail of his face as he locked eyes with me in the moment after he heard the click.

'Not too much. Leave some for tomorrow. If you drain it, it will be gone.'

I snapped awake. The voices were back. It was just the same as before in the bar; the voice appearing inside my head as if I was wearing earphones except I could tell it hadn't come through my ears, plus this time I had a good idea what it was. Yet again, I could feel where they were as if there was a compass in my head telling me which way to go.

I reached to the lamp at the side of my bed and flicked it on. I knew what I was about to do would be considered ridiculous, but I was going to do it anyway. My need to protect people was something I could feel deep down inside myself, like it had always been there and was the driver for joining the army. I felt a flicker of a memory, as elusive as a rabbit in a forest, seen from the corner of your eye but gone by the time you look.

Wincing against the aches I felt from the fight earlier, I crunched my abs to get myself sitting upright. I needed to find someone so I could tell them about what I was hearing.

They needed to investigate. It was coming from beneath me somewhere, which confused me for a moment until I realised the hospital probably had several floors.

Slowly, I swivelled around so my butt was on the edge of the bed. My right leg dangled a few inches lower than my left, the prosthetic taken off for the night so I could sleep more comfortably. I reached for it, but the voice came again.

'If it dies, there will always be another one tomorrow. Human children are always getting sick.'

Children!

The voices, guttural sounds in my head, wouldn't shut off. Their incessance forcing me to steel myself and grit my teeth before sliding down to put my right foot on the floor. The linoleum tile was cold against my skin, though I would pay to feel the same coolness against the bottom of my left foot again. Putting my fake foot on would take me minutes. If I had two hands, I could do it in seconds probably, but with one hand, it was awkward. I didn't have time for the foot, and the hand took far too long to connect, so I left that too.

As the voices rasped again, arguing about who or what they were going to devour, I blew out a hard breath of determination and hopped to the door. It was closed and because it opened from the left side, I had to balance on one foot and lean against the wall to open it cack-handed with my right arm.

Instinctively, as it swung open, I put out my left arm to stop it, the edge of the door striking the very tip of my stump to send a shockwave of pain through me. My head swam and I thought for a moment that I might vomit. The need to empty my stomach was eased by having very little in it, but I still had to wait thirty seconds for the pain to dissipate a little before I could move again.

Across the ward, another door lay open, the tail end of the bed inside visible and the very thing I needed propped against it: a pair of crutches. I could only use one, and I couldn't use it on the left side where I wanted it to replace my missing left foot because I had no left hand to hold it with.

'Goodness, what are you doing out of bed?' Small hands, those of a young woman, gripped my shoulders on either side. She wanted to guide me back to my room. 'Do you need the toilet? There's a call button by your bed.'

'No,' I protested. 'There's...' I wanted to say I could hear voices, but it didn't sound like a clever thing to admit. 'I thought I heard something. Is everyone else okay?' I asked, though I knew it sounded weak.

The nurse steered me back toward my room, then saw how difficult that was going to be with me hopping on one leg. 'Let's get you into a chair,' she said as she let go with one hand to grab a plastic chair from beside the bed. There were two of them for the sleeping resident's visitors to sit on. With an arm behind my back and another holding my right hand, she lowered me into the chair. I didn't want to sit down, but I was certain I knew what her next move would be and needed her to take it. 'I'll be just one moment while I fetch a wheelchair. Just shout if you need me.'

The moment she left the room, I used my right leg and my right arm to push and pull myself back to upright, snagged a crutch and in an awful, awkward hopping, skipping motion, I set off to find the source of the whispers in my head.

I had to hurry so that I would reach the end of the ward and escape before the nurse returned. Finding, when I looked, that my room was mercifully close to the double doors, meant I was able to do just that. The doors were automatic, operated by a push button on the wall, another bonus because I wasn't sure how many more doors I could open for myself. I had been upright for about three minutes and felt like collapsing already. I was tired and sore but if I felt like giving up, the nasty whispers in my head spurred me on.

Leaning against the wall to get my breath and rest, I spotted an elevator. A pair of them, in fact; the giant ones you get in hospitals so patients on beds would fit. However, just to push the call button to get the doors open was a complicated manoeuvre. It involved crossing the corridor and leaning against the wall so I could put the crutch down without dropping it. Then it was necessary to balance on one foot so I could push the button, but I couldn't take my head off the wall as that was what was keeping me steady.

The elevator began moving, I could hear it coming up from one of the floors below. As I waited impatiently for it to arrive, I noticed the blood forming on the end of my left arm stump. Where the door hit it had jarred something loose. Whatever it was, it was going to be unpopular with the doctors in the morning.

I didn't care. It was insignificant. The elevator chimed just as the door began to open. It was empty, which I expected since it wasn't moving when I called it, though now I had to hope I would alight on a floor as quiet as this one. I hadn't looked at the clock in my room, so I didn't know what time it was. It felt like the very early hours though, two or three, where on wards like these, people would be sleeping, and staff would be a skeleton crew.

I had to guess which floor I wanted. I got a general direction from the whispers in my head, but height above ground wasn't included in the package, which meant I had to stop at each floor until, on the third attempt, I knew I had it right. I could feel them, right ahead of me. However, I was looking at a solid wall and had to find doors to get inside.

It was the children's ward; the doors had a painted crocodile with a beaming smile on them in case a person had any doubt, but I couldn't get in. There was a light shining just through the doors at a nurses' station where two women sat in front of computers.

'Quickly, quickly. Don't take too much. Move on to the next one.'

I hammered on the door using my forehead to keep my balance and must have looked demented given the faces on the two women when they looked up in shock.

They exchanged a glance and one rushed across to the doors as the other picked up the phone. Using a card to swipe the door open, the nurse, a woman in her thirties with ample hips and pudgy forearms looked angry that I was creating a disturbance.

'You can't be here,' she growled at me, clearly intending to send me away. Then she saw my missing parts and caught me as I fell forward.

'You have someone in here attacking the children!' I blurted.

'Quickly, quickly, enough for everyone, don't wake them.' They were feeding on the children the same way they had fed on the homeless man and then me.

'Someone's here.' Another blurted, hearing the racket I was making.

There were multiple voices, all of them talking over one another in their excitement and giving the impression they were salivating as if sitting down to a sumptuous meal. Now they fell quiet, listening to hear if they were to be disturbed.

'Nonsense,' the nurse argued. 'Who are you? Why are you out of bed?' Then she turned and called to her colleague. 'Trisha, get security down here.'

'Who do you think I'm talking to now?' Trisha asked, then turned her attention back to the phone. 'Yes. Yes. Just send a couple of men and a wheelchair. No, it's nothing, just a patient out of bed. She looks delirious.'

'Look,' I insisted as Trisha put the phone back into its cradle. 'You need to go and look at the children. There is something in here.'

Stretching ahead of us was a corridor with doors to the left and right. In each of the rooms would be multiple children and I could hear the creatures talking in my head. Mercifully, just as the nurses were about to argue with me, a small sound drew their attention.

'I'm going to check it out,' said Trisha.

The one holding me in place said, 'Just give me a hand first, okay. Can you grab that chair?' she nodded her head toward a wheeled chair in front of a computer which Trisha dutifully brought to her before setting off into the ward.

'Be careful,' I called after her, but my shout didn't help as she looked my way just as she drew level with a door and wasn't looking inside it when she should have been. One of the creatures stepped into the corridor, grabbed a fistful of Trisha's hair and yanked her off her feet. She vanished into the room with a scream that was cut off half a second later.

The nurse with me screamed, then buzzed herself out of the door and ran away.

35

I watched her vanish down the corridor, unable to come up with anything to say other than, 'Perfect.' My flippant remark was made out loud which instantly drew the attention of the creatures still on the ward.

'How many?'

'Just one and it is injured.'

'Not as sweet as the little ones, but a meal nevertheless.'

'Show yourself,' I growled, trying to get back to my feet. The crutch was five feet away where Trisha had placed it against a wall. I had to hop across to it. I didn't want them to see how weak I was, but it was too late for that.

'It can hear us.'

The latest voice sounded worried, its comment causing a confusing torrent of back and forth as they discussed me.

'Show yourself,' I repeated. A foolish request because that was what it did, a lone figure stepping out of the darkness to face me. It sniffed the air as it came forward just like the one in the courtyard had done.

'You are human?' it questioned, its rasping voice confused at the concept. I was about to answer when it stepped into a patch of moonlight coming through a window. Just like the pair in the courtyard, it was ugly as all sin, beady reptilian eyes staring at me as it tried to work out what it was looking at. Ironically that was exactly what I was doing to it. It had on human clothing, jeans and a t-shirt with a leather jacket over the top.

I hadn't answered its question but more of them joined the first one now. Coming out of the shadows where they were expertly hidden like a national hide and seek squad. A quick head count told me there were at least six that I could see.

'Is it a wizard?' one asked, trepidation evident when it spoke.

The first one, who one might guess was the leader, if such a hierarchy existed, shook its head. 'No. It is not drawing on a ley line.' It sniffed deeply again in demonstration. 'It is an ordinary human, and it is weak. This one you can drain. It smells close to death anyway.'

'What are you?' I managed but I was having to grit my teeth against the pain I felt. Balancing on one leg, even with a crutch to help me, wasn't doing me any good. I was so poorly balanced I was going to fall down if I didn't sit down soon, but there was no option for that and just like before, I was about to get attacked and now there were more of them.

No sooner did I acknowledge the likelihood of attack than I sensed them decide to do so. The leader's voice was a whisper, but his instruction to kill me all they needed to get them moving. I wanted to run, but I couldn't and all I had was a crutch to defend myself. Earlier I had killed them with blast of energy from my hand but how had I done that? How had I created it and where the hell did it come from? I needed it now but had no idea how to make it happen so screaming in defiance as they rushed me, I brought the crutch up to swing as a bat, trying desperately to stay on my one good foot. There was nothing in the swing though; it was caught by the first of them as it advanced and a shove was all it took to knock me backward to sprawl painfully on the cold tile. A shockwave of pain sent fire through me as my left arm struck the ground, but then I spotted a person.

Ten feet behind the advancing creatures, a man had appeared as if from nowhere. No one else had seen him yet, but I lost sight of him as one of the things followed me down to the floor. It was coming for me, hungry noises dominating its thoughts as its face drew nearer. It was as if it wanted to kiss me but I knew what it intended. I fought back, anger and frustration manifesting as rage as I struggled against the creature. Then the static electricity thing started to happen again and this time I knew what to do.

The creature placed a knee on my stomach to keep me in place, pinning my waist down with its weight, then pulled out a black knife to threaten me with. It was just like the ones the creatures had used earlier but that was another insignificant detail if I was about to get stabbed with it. Holding it in its left hand, it grabbed my left forearm with its right hand and loomed above me, its face beginning to descend as I saw an opening and thrust my right hand upward.

The static electricity sensation welled up, sparks dancing along my arm as they travelled down to my hand. I had enough time to see the creature's face rear back in shock before a ball of light filled my palm and blasted outward from it.

The brightness of the blast forced my eyes shut, but when I opened them again, the creature's head was missing just like before. The remains of the body fell backwards away from me, the weight, which had been pinning me down, now lifting away as it dissipated into the air as dust.

How I was producing the orbs of light blue energy was of no concern so long as I could keep doing it. It was the strangest sensation, the energy welling up from inside my body. Looking at my right arm, the hairs were settling again, the static electricity gone but I felt confident to be able to do it at will now. Using my left elbow to push my upper half off the floor, I found every single one of the creatures were staring at me. There had to be at least a half a dozen of them. I didn't know what the blue bolt of energy thing was, but it sure got their attention.

Unified by their fear, the creatures all rushed me at once. With a yelp of shock in reaction to their charge, I threw my right hand up in self-defence. Nothing happened this time. At least, nothing happened with strange balls of light shooting from my palm. What did happen was the creatures swarmed all over me.

They were grabbing my limbs to pin them down and the pain I felt from my ruined arm and leg was terrible. I couldn't begin to describe it if I tried, but my consciousness swam and threatened to shut me down as I tried to fight them off. My head was pinned suddenly, at least one pair of hands grabbing my hair to hold me in place. When a gap appeared between the creatures, the man I saw a moment ago was still there, watching me with a surprised expression. He wasn't coming to my aid, though. He was just watching. He could have at least yelled for help. It made me mad but before I could channel that emotion into something productive, one of the creatures put its mouth down to my face and a glow began to shine from its mouth. This time I knew what it was; I knew what was happening and I knew I had to work out how to make the energy thing appear.

Still pinned, I could barely move. The pain like lava in my veins hit me again, however, I was able to focus my thoughts and that allowed me to think about what I had done when

I made the ball of light appear in my hand. Had I even made it appear? Was it something I did? Or was it something that happened by itself? I closed my eyes again and shut out the feeling of having my energy sucked out while I searched myself for a way to do it again.

What had I been doing? Trying to protect myself. That was the only answer I had, but I had been in fight situations before and never pushed a ball of deadly light from my hand. I gave up trying to work out how I had done it and opened the palm of my right hand. The instant I thought about forming the energy ball in my hand, I felt the same sensation of static electricity channelling down my arm.

With a savage mental fist pump, I aimed my hand at the creature sucking on my neck and fired a pulse of death straight into it. The feeling of having my energy sapped stopped instantly. I was free to attack, and I was fired up now so nothing was going to stop me.

Another of the creatures leapt for my right arm, trying to pin it down but my palm was open so it got a face full of light and as its body turned to dust a moment later, I looked down my own chest as I lay on the floor and fired another shot and then another.

The man became visible again as the next creature became dust. He had moved closer and looked like he was coming to help me but hadn't got that far yet. His face was still registering shock, his shaggy blonde hair reminded me of a stereotypical surfer dude, someone who might say, 'Cool,' a lot. I thought for a moment he was going to wade in and try to save me, but as I struggled to get my right arm around to kill another of the freakish beasts, he stepped back once more, leaving me to manage without his assistance. I took my eyes off him to fire a bolt into another of the monsters, and when I looked back, he was no longer there. Where he had been, the air had an odd shimmer to it for no more than a heartbeat before it too was gone.

I had no time to focus on what I might have seen; I was still trying to survive the pack of things I disturbed feeding on the children. They had scurried into cover, escaping me by diving behind the nurses' station. To get the rest of them I would have to find a way to walk.

'What are you?' one of them hissed, peering around the edge of the desk then ducking back as I threw another orb of light at it. The shot missed and hit the far wall where it left a scorch mark. Everything hurt and my head was pounding. The brain surgeon, and everyone since, had told me to avoid blows to my head. I wasn't doing too well at obeying that instruction tonight. They were still here though, so I had to find the effort required to get across to the desk. I let my latest ball of energy recede into my hand before trying to lever myself up on the wheeled chair.

It gave the creatures the brief respite they needed. Only two remained and they chose that moment to make themselves visible by standing up. I turned to fire a shot at them, but a circle of shimmering air grew behind them to a size of roughly two yards before the survivors stepped backward through it to vanish before my eyes.

I continued to gawp at the space where they had been. They were gone though, as was the man with the surfer hair, and now I really felt spent. I needed to get up and check on the children. I needed to see if any of them were hurt, but as I tried to get up, I slipped on my own blood. Both my stumps were bleeding, and I could feel a stickiness on my forehead where I had sustained a cut. This time, as I fell back, I allowed myself a moment to recover.

But then I heard the doors behind me fly open, slamming against their stops as people rushed in. Shouting voices filled the air, making me curse the sky and everything in it as I accepted the fight wasn't over, but before I could form another ball of energy, I saw people swarming around me; real people, not hideous creatures, the nurse who fled was among them.

I had no fight left anyway, no ability to help the children or see if any of them were hurt, but the people passing me now were doing those things for me. Hands were on me, human hands and I accepted there was nothing more I could do.

The nurses fussed around me, checking my wounds and asking me what had happened. Beyond them, the security guards were shouting to each other and we all heard their cry when they found Trisha's body.

I couldn't think of anything to say. I had a feeling I was going to be seeing Detective Sergeant Spencer sooner than either one of us wanted, but as the nurses lifted me off the floor and onto a hospital bed someone brought over, my mind was focused on the face of the man who had been watching the attack. What was his part in this? He wasn't surprised by the creatures, he acted as if they were an everyday event. There had been surprise on his face though; surprise at me.

Unanswered questions were stacking up in my head but the one at the front wasn't one I thought up. It was one the creature asked: 'What are you?'

Chapter 6

They took me back to my room and settled me in bed. A doctor came by a short while later while a pair of nurses were dressing the left leg stump. I had caught it at some point during the fight and made the wound from the courtyard fight even worse. I had a couple of other scrapes but not ones I would bother to list.

The doctor was more concerned about my head and the piece of shrapnel inside it. As he shone a light into my eyes, first the right and then the left, he asked, 'Do you have any blurring to your vision now or in the last hour?'

'No.'

'Any nausea?

'No.'

He held up a pen for me to track with my eyes. As it went back and forth, he asked, 'Did the army surgeons advise you to avoid blows to the head?'

I snorted a laugh. 'Yes, they did. I would very happily avoid getting hit in the head if I could.'

'What happened on the children's ward?' He seemed to be satisfied that the sliver of steel in my brain wasn't about to cause an embolism and had turned off his pen light. Now he was studying me as if I was a curiosity of some sort.

I didn't know how to answer his question without lining myself up for a psychiatric review. Instead, I asked. 'Are the children okay?'

He blinked a couple of times as if considering how to answer, but then said, 'Yes. Several of them have the same weird mark on their neck as you, though. What caused it?'

Tricky ground. That's where I found myself. But as I thought of a lie I might tell, rescue came in the unlikely form of Detective Sergeant Spencer. He appeared in the doorway, drawing everyone's attention, including mine, without even speaking.

Once we were looking at him, he asked, 'Are you nearly done? I need to interview her.'

The doctor moved out of the way and back toward the door. 'Quite done, thank you.'

'Will I be discharged in the morning?' I called after him as DS Spencer stood back to let him out.

He paused with one hand on the door frame and his feet already in the corridor. 'That decision will be made by the consultant. However, I currently see no medical reason to keep you here.' Silently, the nurses packed up their gear and left too.

DS Spencer waited patiently for them all to leave and then ambled into the room, looked about for a chair to sit on, and just like in the emergency department, settled into it with his notebook and pen ready. 'Now then, Miss Aaronson, what was it I said earlier about not seeing you again?'

'Hardly my fault.'

'A nurse was killed on the children's ward, Miss Aaronson. She has the same mark on her neck as the previous victim and so do some of the children. And so do you. I think you should tell me why you went to the children's ward in the middle of the night, disturbed the two nurses there and how it is that you knew something was going on.'

I drew in a breath through my nose. The nurse who survived; the one who ran away, must have already been questioned and told them about the crazy woman with missing limbs hammering to be let in. Did I dare to tell him the truth?

43

I shrugged mentally and gave it my best shot. 'I hear voices in my head.' As soon as I said the words I stopped talking. I sounded like a crazy person. I hear voices in my head was a bumper slogan. DS Spencer's face hadn't changed at all and he was waiting silently for me to say more. I tried again. 'The children were being attacked by monsters of some kind.'

'Nurse Shaw said she saw a man.'

'A man?' I questioned. Then I remembered something one of them said back at the courtyard. He said I could see through their enchantments. I had no idea what that meant but I saw a way to get out of this now and started lying through my teeth. 'I was sore lying in bed, and I hadn't had any dinner, between one thing and another it just didn't happen today, so I went in search of a vending machine. I got lost and got off on the wrong floor and walked past the children's ward. I saw the man going into one of the rooms, so I shouted to get the attention of the two nurses at their station and you know what happened after that.'

DS Spencer didn't look up straight away, he finished writing what I had told him and then looked to be rereading it. 'What did you mean when you said you hear voices in your head?'

I pointed to the scar on my face. 'You already know I have a piece of shrapnel in there; sometimes I think it picks up radio channels.' I tried a smile, hoping I could give him the impression I was a little crazy but completely harmless. It was that or I was going to have to tell him about the creatures I had seen and fought twice now and that would lead to me proving the story by creating an orb of blue energy in my right hand. I doubted that strategy would work out well for me.

I could hear him breathing. It was still dark out, though most of the night was done, but people on the ward were sleeping, and it was quiet. He was looking down at his notes again.

'I don't believe you.' His statement was a simple one, but it carried a lot of meaning. Instantly angry at being called a liar even though I was lying, I felt my face form a frown as I opened my mouth to retort. He held a hand up to stop me and stood up, speaking over me before I could say anything. 'However, just as before, the witnesses and the victims, in this case the children, describe men as their attackers, not you. If you know who is doing this, Miss Aaronson, it would be a crime for you to not tell me. That is known as aiding and abetting. This is now a murder enquiry and I have little patience for your lies.' Yet again, as I opened my mouth to argue, he spoke over me. 'If you are wondering how I know you are lying, it is very simple, Miss Aaronson: I am observant. You had to walk past vending machines directly outside your ward when you left it and when you arrived at the children's ward you didn't have a purse or handbag or any money with you.'

My cheeks flushed at how easily he had picked apart my story.

He produced a card from his wallet and placed it, the right way up for me to read, on the bed in front of me. 'You may be innocent of attacking anyone, Miss Aaronson, but I believe I will be seeing you again very soon.'

Then he left, strolling out of the door and turning right as he took a packet of cigarettes out of his jacket pocket.

Exhausted, I put my head back to stare at the ceiling and shortly I slept.

Chapter 7

Geographically not that far from where Anastasia slept, but in an altogether different plane of reality, immortal wizard, Otto Schneider, faced down a man he badly wanted to kill. Sean McGuire was a traitor to the human race for a start, but his crimes against Otto were far more personal than that. Neither man had ever heard the name Anastasia Aaronson, and though they soon would, now was not the time for anything other than fighting.

The ground heaved as Otto wrenched a huge ball of dirt from it to throw at his opponent. It had to weigh two tons or more and came as one lump, like a giant boulder hurled from a trebuchet. Across the field, his opponent sucked ley line energy into his body to power his own spell, conjuring an invisible wall of air to sweep the ball from the sky.

Its trajectory altered, moving left so it would collide harmlessly with the ground to his right, but once it was safely diverted, Sean pushed a new conjuring into it, manipulating the air to make it spin. As the giant clod became debris within a tornado, it began to break apart, pieces the size of house bricks flying off from it as he turned it around and sent it back.

Sean, a wizard of Irish descent and the familiar of a powerful demon, had never fought his opponent before, but he had wanted to for a long time. Most of the demons would spit when his name was ever mentioned and with good reason. Otto Schneider had caused more trouble and wrought more damage to their plans than any being in over four millennia. Every demon in the immortal realm wanted Otto dead but they couldn't kill him and he knew it, so he was on the offensive, attacking them when anyone else would be cowering in a hole and hoping to die before the death curse failed and the demons could return to Earth.

Sean's tornado looked like a twisting finger of death to him, he had never conjured one more deadly. To control it on its course, he manipulated the air and pushed it onwards. Otto looked unperturbed though, choosing to propel himself upward with an air spell which he used to fly around the twister. Sean could reverse the tornado's direction but then it would be heading for him again. Dropping it was the obvious option, but before he could consider which elemental magic to employ next, Otto dropped from the sky, releasing the air spell that kept him aloft so he could fire lightning downwards.

The first strike hit the ground near Sean's feet, blasting him off them to land in a heap ten yards away. The magically imbued lightning earthed through clothing designed to take the punishment, but it still hurt like hell.

'You will not kill again!' bellowed Otto in English, his heavy German accent easy to detect. 'Wherever you hide, I will find you,' he added as he manipulated more air to slow his descent and touch lightly onto the ground.

Sean sneered, 'Who is hiding? I am right here, Schneider, and there will be nowhere for *you* to hide when the death curse fails.' Keeping a lightning spell of his own ready, he waited to see what Otto might do next. Daniel had to be here somewhere. He, more than anyone else, wanted to tear Otto apart. The demons planned to trap him and keep him in a state where he could do no more harm. So far, all their attempts to capture him on Earth had failed, but here he was, already in the immortal realm. If Sean could keep him distracted, maybe this would be his master's chance.

Sean was surprised when Otto didn't follow up his lightning strike with another, or with something else. Thrown off balance, Sean was an easy target to pick off. Had the positions been reversed, Otto would now be immobilised. Sean got to his feet. His long coat, imbued with magic to act as a barrier, was still functional though its effectiveness would be reduced by the impact of Otto's spells. He eyed the German wizard warily from the depths of his cowl, calculating which attack he should employ next. Otto was clearly waiting for him to make the next move.

In a flurry of hand movements, he threw a jet of flame across the field, anticipated which way Otto might attempt to flee and tried to get there first. As the flame, hot enough to cut through steel, tore towards his opponent, Sean readied his next spell, a manipulation of air which he thrust outward behind the flame so it might not be detected until too late.

It was ironic that he had learned this spell from Otto himself, seeing him use it on another familiar many months ago.

The flame struck Otto's barrier, a conjuring of air and energy that produced a magical barrier he had seen the wizard use to deflect hellfire, the demons' primary weapon and one which would kill a human on contact. Any human except Otto Schneider that is. The barrier spell burned out under the onslaught of the flame, but a new barrier would follow it instantly - Sean knew Otto's tactics well enough. That is why he used the asphyxiation spell, a simple manipulation of air that cut off the ability for the victim to draw breath.

It had no physical form, unlike fire or lightning, so it caught Otto by surprise as it shut off his supply of oxygen.

Seeing it take hold, the moment of shock on Otto's face and then his focus on trying to break the spell, gave Sean a fleeting sense of victory. Otto could throw whatever he wanted at him now because all Sean had to do was keep the air spell in place for a few more seconds. They were both out of breath; adrenalin from fighting and the sheer effort of conjuring spell after spell was enough to make anyone breathless, but Sean's sense of triumph lasted only as long as it took Otto to conjure the exact same spell.

Sean should have expected it; should have expected something, but his senses were all attuned to an attack with lightning or earth, not the clever sneak attack Otto employed. The feeling of not being able to draw breath was an awful one, it was only seconds before he could feel his pulse hammering in his chest. Gritting his teeth, he held on, maintaining his own hold on Otto's air supply and trusting the German would lose consciousness first.

His vision was starting to get spotty as he watched Otto for signs that he was fading. Then, he went down to one knee while Sean remained upright. He was going to win, but his vision was fading, and he was going to lose consciousness if he didn't breathe very soon.

He too, had to get closer to the ground, his head banging now as the sound of his pulse became the only thing he could hear.

To an observer, it would have looked as if both lost at the same time. In actuality, Otto lost consciousness first, but Sean was so close behind him that it made no difference to the outcome. Then it became a race to see who would get up first as the oxygen flooded back into their bodies.

Sean's head ached terribly, that was the dominant thought as he opened his eyes, but the memory of the fight flooded in a half heartbeat later, adrenalin surging back into his bloodstream as urgent messages to get up and fight forced him to face where Otto had been.

Otto Schneider was already standing. The sight caused Sean to freeze, using caution to prolong the fight as it was clear his opponent had the upper hand.

'The demons will not win,' said Otto. His hands were up and ready to cast but he had made no attempt to kill Sean while he was down, choosing to talk instead. Why hadn't Otto finished him?

Sean couldn't stop himself from laughing. 'Really, Otto? You think the angels can over-come them? They are outnumbered twenty to one.'

'The angels will not win either.'

'Who will then?' Both men swung their heads in the direction of the new voice just as Beelzebub stepped into view, his entourage right behind him. They were in a clearing, but there were boulders at the periphery and trees which had done the task of concealing the massive demon's approach. Now Sean understood why Otto hadn't cast a final spell to end his life: he knew Beelzebub would intervene. 'Will it be Otto Schneider?' the demon ruler asked.

Sean, knelt, getting one knee to the ground and bowing his head as he knew he must. There was no longer any need to fight his opponent; there were twenty demons approach-ing. Among them was Daniel, Sean's master, and once the master of Otto Schneider. De-spite the problems Otto caused and his subsequent fall from grace, Daniel had managed to maintain his position in Beelzebub's inner circle. How long he stayed there now came down to the success of his next plan. Whatever it was, Sean would be only too pleased to help him enact it though he was quite content to continue tracking down and killing the familiar Otto had recently freed.

Risking a glance at the German wizard, Sean saw him scan along the line of demons emerging from the treeline. It looked to Sean as if the wizard were trying to decide whether to attack them or not. Surely, he couldn't be that crazy, but as he wondered what he might do, he saw the wizard reach out to his rear with his left hand and conjure a portal. Otto narrowed his eyes at the demon ruler and stepped backward to vanish, returning to the mortal realm where he would choose a destination in daylight, knowing the demons could not follow.

It was a known fact that humans could not conjure a portal. None ever had since the realms were split more than four thousand years ago, but Otto Schneider, a wizard with no more than a couple of decades of adult life behind him, had worked out how to do it. It infuriated and frustrated Sean, his own ability as a wizard recognised as among the most powerful in the immortal realm, but somehow insignificant when compared to a man a quarter of his age.

Like all the familiars, he was given demon blood to sustain him. It stopped them from aging so on his one hundred and sixtieth birthday, he looked the same as he had when Daniel first came to him in County Kildare. Aged just twenty-six, he was frozen in time and would be until the death curse failed.

Beelzebub and his followers were departing, the woodland seemingly absorbing them as they vanished into it. Only Daniel remained, and watching him from the edge of the trees, Nathaniel, one of the most senior demons and one who held a grudge against Daniel.

Daniel had found Sean and brought him to the immortal realm where he trained him before handing him to Nathaniel. When Daniel's familiar was killed by Otto, the demon claimed the wizard as his new familiar only to discover that he could not be controlled. Beelzebub had allowed Daniel to convince him that he needed Sean under his control in order to rectify issues Otto had caused and despite Nathaniel's protests, the deal had gone ahead. Now Nathaniel was without a familiar and very unhappy about it.

Sean rose from his kneeling position to meet his master. Daniel said, 'It is time to move forward, Sean.' A human might have asked him if he was okay after the battle with Otto, but that wasn't in a demon's makeup. 'Some shilt were attacked a few hours ago in the mortal realm. Several were killed.' Sean didn't react; no one cared much for the shilt. They were base creatures only tolerated because they made good foot soldiers. Some quirk in their DNA meant they were able to travel between realms more easily than any other species so Daniel used them to do his dirty work in turn for treating them better than the other demons did. 'They reported a human girl who was able to wield source energy.'

The significance of his master's statement shocked him. 'But that means ...'

'What it means,' Daniel cut across him, 'is that we have no time to lose. Or rather, you have no time to lose. The shilt know better than to lie or embellish their stories so there must be some truth to the report. Find the girl, stay as long as you need and use her to locate the artefact. If I am right, then this is the move that will see me ascend to Beelzebub's right hand and that will guarantee you the fiefdom you desire when we reclaim Earth.'

Keeping his excitement in check, Sean asked, 'Where is she?'

'England. In a small city called Rochester. At least, that is where she killed the shilt just a few hours ago. Get there, find her, and bring her to me.'

'How will I return here once I have her?'

Daniel nodded at the pertinent question. 'I am sending the shilt with you. As many as you need. Use them to distract the mortals. I have enlisted an ogre to lead them, but they will do your bidding as if it were mine.' Daniel gripped his familiar's shoulder. 'No one else knows of this yet. We must keep it that way. My rivals will attempt to claim the prize for themselves. Even Beelzebub himself may choose to dispatch warriors to obtain the armour if he knows it can be achieved. I gain nothing if another gets to her first.'

'Very good, master. I must prepare.' Then he paused as a question occurred to him. 'What of my other task, master? Eliminating the freed familiars?'

'This takes priority, but if you have the chance to kill a familiar, do so. They are wise to resist using their magic, knowing it would lead us to them, but we must eliminate them all before the death curse fails, they are too capable to be left alive.'

Daniel walked away, following the route the other demons had taken and Sean followed behind. He had been born the son of a poverty-stricken potato farmer one hundred and sixty-four years ago at the end of Ireland's potato famine. His father survived, though his mother did not, but life had been a struggle until his abilities manifested and soon after that Daniel came for him. Soon, he would rule a fiefdom within Daniel's kingdom and though he would finally start ageing, his life would be filled with riches and banquets his ancestors could never have imagined. All he had to do was find the woman and bring her back to Daniel in the immortal realm without the other demons knowing.

It was going to be easy.

Chapter 8

I t was almost ten and the consultant still hadn't made his rounds. I was bored but I wasn't in a great rush to leave. My boss at the library, an old professor called Gershwin Grayhawk who I had spoken to on the phone but never met, told me I should take the rest of the week off. I was to be his research assistant, but he had managed without for this long he said, and, in his opinion, I needed to rest and recover. I thanked him but expressed my belief that I would find it cathartic to establish a routine. Truthfully, I was keen to get to work; Zannaria was a long time ago now and I had been in hospital ever since. In fact, I thought it cruelly ironic that I was back in one now just a day after finally being discharged.

However, I couldn't claim that thoughts of work, or anything normal, filled my mind this morning. In two separate incidents yesterday, I heard, found, and then fought creatures that were either aliens from another planet or some kind of supernatural monster. I didn't know which and found both concepts laughable. It might even have been funny if I hadn't created something magical too.

I sat on the bed and closed my eyes to concentrate. The voices were clear and unavoidable last night but there was no trace of them now. Would they return? I watched them vanish into thin air on the children's ward last night and I fired blasts of magical blue energy from my right hand which killed them and caused their bodies to turn to dust. I needed to talk to someone about it, but who could I even raise the subject with?

A memory of the man standing behind the ugly reptilian creatures resurfaced. Who the hell was he? He looked human and would be able to answer my questions, though if I ever saw him again, the first thing I would do would be to punch his face.

The list of questions in my head was getting longer. Had he been there to control them? His shaggy blonde hair and blue eyes were features I would remember. But then a new question occurred to me. Nurse Shaw saw one of them too right before it grabbed Trisha. However, she claimed she saw a man, and DS Spencer said the children claimed to have seen men and so did the homeless man in his report. It looped me back to the question about an enchantment to hide their features. If that was the case, then why did I see them as they truly are?

Magic.

I looked down at my right hand, then nervously across at the door. Then I hopped off the bed to get to the little en-suite toilet, glad that one of the nurses had helped me get my left foot back on earlier so I could avoid the struggle for one day. Safely tucked inside, I focused on what I had done earlier, closing my eyes to imagine forming the ball of light in my hand and opened them again as I felt the energy begin to crackle over my skin.

I stopped. Was this magic? Had the sliver of steel in my brain joined two points that now allowed me to do something no one else could? I tried again, this time with my eyes open and thinking consciously about what I needed to do to create the ball of energy. Arcs of blue light jumped across my skin as I sent the magic (what the hell else was I to call it?) out of my chest and down my arm. In my open palm, a sphere of crackling light blue energy appeared. It wasn't attached to me by anything other than more arcs of the same light blue colour. I could see into it but not through as I held it in front of my face and turned it this way and that.

It was wonderous, but I had no idea what it was. It was destructive though, I had used it to kill ... six times, I counted in my head. Six of the ugly beasts had died from my blasting them with the blue orbs.

'Soul suckers.' I gave them a name, saying it out loud to see how it sounded. I was mentally referring to them as creatures or beasts because I had no name for them, but soul sucker worked much better.

'Everything alright in there?' The toilet door rattled as someone outside tried to get in.

The voice made me jump and I shot the blue orb into the ceiling tiles where it burnt a round hole.

'I'm coming in!' announced the voice outside, a worried nurse or orderly no doubt, and I could hear them fumbling for a key to open the door from the outside.

Quickly I flushed the toilet, shouting, 'Won't be a moment,' before opening the door and shutting it again quickly so they couldn't see the damage to the ceiling.

The orderly, a young, pretty Asian woman, looked startled. 'Is everything, okay? she asked. 'There was all kinds of light coming from around the doorframe; I thought maybe there was a fire.'

I feigned a laugh. 'I was watching a movie trailer on my phone. It was for a new sci-fi film. Lots of laser blasts and such.'

The woman looked a little sceptical but didn't argue. 'I came to clean the room.'

'Do you need me out of the way?'

'No, miss. No, no. Nothing like that. You make yourself comfortable. I'll just clean around you.' She bustled about for a few minutes, efficiently cleaning everything there was to clean with sprays and wipes and disposable cloths. I sat in a chair in the corner and thought about what I had been witness to. There were articles on the internet, lots of them, far too many for me to read, that was for sure. But as I tried to pick between the blatantly made up and the possibly real, I found lots of conspiracy theory suggesting that the things I saw last night had been seen elsewhere before. There were even drawings; artists impressions I think you would call them. It was enough to convince me I wasn't the first to ever see the soul suckers. I read other reports where people described the same shimmering pool of air I saw last night. One was in Haiti, the report one of many compiled on a website called Demon Tracker. The woman making the report claimed she was attacked with her boyfriend who was then subdued by two large men before being dragged through the shimmering air to vanish before her eyes. She had never seen him again.

The website's author claimed to have found more than two hundred examples of people being kidnapped in the same manner and posited that it was the work of aliens coming to us from a parallel dimension.

My reading was interrupted by the consultant arriving. She was a Japanese woman with an American accent and round glasses with thick lenses that distorted her face when I looked directly at it. She had a gaggle of junior doctors with her and talked about me as if I were a science experiment as she told them what she knew of my medical history and injuries. It was several minutes before she spoke to me directly.

The upshot was that I was discharged, not that I had any plan to stay, but she had no reason to keep me.

On my way out of the ward, one of the nurses stopped me. I tried to remember her first name, but it wouldn't come. 'Did I forget something?' I asked, wondering if I was supposed to sign out or something before leaving.

'No. I wanted to let you know there was a man looking for you. I thought maybe he was here to give you a lift at first, but I don't think he was because he didn't know your name.'

'What do you mean?'

Helen – I remembered her name – pulled me to one side so we weren't blocking the corridor. 'I was collecting something from the reception desk when he came in. He had on weird clothes for a start, not that it's a crime to dress differently, but his coat was almost floor length and he had his hood up to hide his face. Anyway, he was asking for the woman who battled the shilt.'

'The shilt?'

'Yes. Karen on reception said the same thing. I figured we had all misheard him, but he said it again. He wanted to find the woman who battled the shilt last night. Then he said it had happened on the children's ward and I knew he meant you.'

I glanced around wondering if he was here somewhere. 'Where is he now?'

'With security. Karen called them. Like I said – he was weird looking and wouldn't put his hood down. I just thought you should know in case it was someone you knew.'

Someone was here looking for me. I didn't like the sound of that, and I certainly didn't want to meet whoever it was. I thanked her and got her to show me a safe way out that would avoid the main entrance and limit the likelihood of running into whoever he was.

It was sunny outside, and not too cold, the midday early October temperature a balmy twenty centigrade as England enjoyed an Indian summer. Professor Gershwin Grayhawk wasn't expecting me today, but I was going to the library anyway. I wanted to see it for a start.

The library building was a big place located toward the south end of the city's ancient High Street. A taxi from outside the hospital dropped me right in front of it but I wasn't going in to meet my new boss and co-workers dressed as I was in scruffy leggings and an oversized hoody. I managed to clean myself up in the hospital, using the little pots of toiletries provided so at least I didn't smell, but I was still wearing yesterday's clothes and that just wouldn't do. There were suits back at the flat in my big box of belongings, but they had been in there for months now. They might have gone in neatly folded, but all the time and effort required to get one ready to wear was, quite frankly, beyond me.

I was going shopping instead.

Fifty minutes later, I had a pile of clothes that were a bit more suitable for a first day at work. Now I just had to get the stupid things on with my one hand. Getting dressed and undressed took skills I was yet to master. I hadn't bothered with a bra since I awoke in the hospital months ago, I just couldn't work out how to do it for myself and had to be thankful my meagre chest didn't need much support. Thick black leggings and a pair of black ankle boots hid my prosthetic left foot well enough. There was a line on my shin about halfway up where the cuff stopped but I was content no one would mention it. A knee-length floral summer dress completed the outfit and I even found a place selling makeup where two girls were more than happy to tidy up my face and hair if I was buying their products. My prosthetic left hand was completely exposed in the halter neck dress, but I was telling myself to embrace what I was and learn to deal with it.

With my old things in a plastic bag and feeling much better about life, I made my way back to the library.

I didn't get there.

Chapter 9

As I turned off the high street and onto Eastgate Terrace, a figure detached itself from the wall it had been nonchalantly leaning against. I would never have noticed if they hadn't moved but now the person was on a path that would intercept mine.

It looked to be a man, which is to say it was man shaped and had big man hands protruding from the sleeves of his coat, but a hood, which might more accurately be called a cowl, was pulled over his head to hide his face quite completely. He was oddly dressed, his coat ending just a few inches from the ground where tan leather boots took over and I knew instantly it was the man who had been trying to find me at the hospital. As he walked, the coat, which was open and loose, showed leather trousers beneath and a coarse tunic on top.

There were other people around, but a quick glance over my shoulder revealed there was no one behind me and thus it was me he was coming toward and no one else.

Curiosity turned to concern as he lifted both his hands and began to move them. My feet slowed and stopped as I glanced around again to see if anyone was watching. Beyond the man were two women sitting on a bench to eat their lunch. They had the look of library workers but neither had noticed what was happening fifteen yards away. Beyond them, the ring road around Rochester flowed by in both directions, but as three people walked in through the library doors, the four of us were the only people left in sight.

'Can I help you?' I asked, becoming annoyed with the man's odd behaviour. He had stopped ten feet from me and was doing something with his left hand while holding his right hand palm upwards.

He didn't answer my question, instead, he swept his left arm around in a flourish and pushed it in my direction. I was slammed backward by an invisible force which picked me up so no part of me was touching the ground until, half a second later, my left elbow clipped the pavement. I tumbled and rolled, the gasps of the two women having their lunch reaching my ears as they saw what happened.

Whatever it was that hit me, knocked me over, but then stopped, so once I finished rolling, I was able to right myself. The man was coming my way, purposeful strides closing the distance as he began swirling his left arm again. His movement was different this time, but I planned to respond in kind.

With a snarl of defiance, I pushed myself upright and focused on visualising the blue energy in my hand. A now familiar sensation of static electricity arcing over my skin began to happen, but the man was too fast for me.

He saw what I was doing, his whole body froze for a split second, but that was all I got before he launched his next attack. Unsure what to expect, it certainly wasn't the sudden inability to breathe. It was as if my lungs had shut off, or my head was suddenly in a vacuum. Panic set in quickly when I tried to draw a breath and could get no air in.

He stalked closer, his right palm still held upward as if he were balancing something on it and his left arm still now as he held it over his right. Whatever was happening to me, he was doing it and my brain, though it was being starved of oxygen, was telling me I was witnessing magic. Real magic, not the illusion stuff on television and very different from what I could do.

It didn't matter what it was because I was about to lose consciousness and had no idea why I was being attacked or who this man was. I couldn't ask him either, not that I thought he was going to tell me, but just as my pulse began hammering in my head to drown out everything else, the spell broke and air flooded back into my lungs.

I gasped in a huge lungful, holding my throat with my one good hand, then saw what had caused the man to stop. One of the women eating her lunch had attacked him and now he was facing her.

I hadn't taken in much detail when I glanced at her earlier, but now I could see that she was huge. Not in a negative way but just overall oversized. The man had to be about six feet tall, but she was at least a couple of inches taller than that. I took all that in as she swung her handbag for a second time.

It was arcing down toward the crown of his skull, but a flick of his hands sent her flying backward as if yanked from behind. Much like I had, she tumbled and rolled, arms and legs flailing and her skirt going over her head to show the world her bum when she crashed into a raised flower bed. The threat from his rear eliminated, the man focused his attention back on me, but the woman had given me the distraction I needed.

With teeth gritted against the reports of pain coming from all over my body and the still thumping pulse as my lungs tried to recover, I pushed power into my right hand and let it go with a shout of indignant outrage, 'You ruined my new dress!'

My scream seemed to surprise him but not as much as the blast from my right hand which evened the score a little as it blasted him backward like a wrecking ball to his chest. It didn't kill him, unlike the soul suckers last night. There was no hole through his chest where it struck, and he wasn't disintegrating like they had.

The blast threw him into the glass front of the library, a resounding thump drawing the attention of those inside. He bounced off and caught himself, his head whipping up to look at me from inside the cowl and I caught my first glimpse of his face, a flash of teeth surrounded by stubble.

Behind him, faces began appearing on the other side of the windows. Curious people with wide-eyes surprised by the sudden noise.

I hadn't readied a second orb, expecting that the first would do it as it had with the soul suckers, but I should have. The man leapt back to his feet, 'So the shilt weren't lying. What are you?' he asked, a distinctly Irish accent giving a lilt to his question. He was already creating another spell, but this time, as he moved his hands, I got to see the air above his head crackling. It fizzed as if I were watching electricity jumping around but as my own eyes widened in a mix of terror and shock, he thrust his hands toward me.

He had created lightning!

In the heartbeat that passed between his hands moving and the lightning bolt striking, I pushed my own magical energy outward from my core to fill my right hand. But I was far too slow to do anything about his attack. I flinched when I felt my hair lifting from the energy coming my way. It shouldn't be possible to see lightning, not up close at least, but I could. It was going to hit me, but at the last moment a man dived in to land by my side and raised his left arm in front of us both like he was holding a shield. He shouted something I didn't understand. It sounded like, 'Cordus,' and a translucent disc appeared inches in front of my nose.

The lightning hit the disc and I got to watch it arc to ground. The shield was ethereal, like a giant umbrella held sideways and it had a blue tinge to it which made it like looking through a piece of blue glass. Around the circumference were symbols I didn't recognise.

My attacker screamed in anger at the new player, then took off running, leaping down to the pavement and firing another pulse of lightning that once again dissipated against the shield.

I had no idea who either man was or what the hell was going on, but before I could speak, the man who came to my defence dropped his shield and chased after the man in the cowl. I only caught a glimpse of him; the lightning attack lasted no more than a couple of seconds and the blinding light from it left glowing coronas in my eyes that made it hard to see. He was tall and thin and in his thirties; his hair and beard were trimmed down to stubble, but when I called after him, I got a proper look at his face.

'Hey! Who are you? What the hell was that shield?' He didn't stop running but turned his head to stare at me before he ran around the corner. He was neither handsome nor ugly, his features all correctly positioned and proportioned but he would fail to stand out in a crowd. What I noted was his pale skin which made me think he lived in a cold climate and his expression was bewildered and filled with questions. He didn't ask any of them, and he didn't slow down as he raced around the corner after my assailant and was gone.

As my heart beat and my legs felt weak from the jolt of adrenalin, there was nothing but silence in the plaza in front of the library. Then the doors burst open and two dozen people spilled from it, some of them coming my way, others running to the tall woman who had righted herself and corrected her skirt. She looked a little dazed and had blood coming from a cut on her head. She was my age, or thereabouts, but I lost sight of her as she was surrounded by people coming to her aid.

'Are you okay?' asked the first man to reach me, a studious looking fellow in his forties. He wore a name badge that told me his name was Professor Duncan Holliman - he worked at the library.

I was bent over with my right hand on my right knee, still trying to get my breath back after the magical throttling I endured. 'I'll live,' I managed between wheezing breaths.

The next person to arrive was another member of the library staff, a woman in her sixties with hair dyed dark brown though it was a few days past needing a refresh as the grey roots were showing through. She wore a woollen twinset with a lump up one sleeve where she had hidden a tissue or handkerchief. 'Are you alright, my dear?' she asked. 'I've called the police; they are on their way right now.' Her name badge said Delores Castle.

The first man asked, 'Do you know who they were?'

'Beats the shit out of me,' I blurted. They were asking how I was, but no one had mentioned the shield the man used to protect me or questioned how I produced a ball of blue energy from my hand that blasted my attacker across the plaza. Had they not seen it?

The older lady seemed a little put out by my choice of phrase, but as more people began to fuss around me, I spotted someone I recognised. I raised my right hand as I called, 'Professor Grayhawk.'

He was checking on the other woman when I called his name, spinning around to see who had addressed him when he heard my shout. We hadn't met so he didn't recognise me when I waved; I knew him from his online biography.

'Hello. Do I know you? Are you alright?' Everyone wanted to ask if I was alright, but I understood why. I already had cuts, bruises and abrasions on the exposed parts of my skin from the two fights yesterday and now my clothing was ripped and marked and I had fresh blood coming from a cut to my left elbow plus yet more cuts and scrapes from tumbling across the stone surface.

Cutting to the chase, I said, 'Hello, Professor. I'm Anastasia Aaronson.'

'Well, my goodness,' he replied, looking stunned. 'I think we had better get you inside.'

Professor Holliman wanted to help me walk but I waved him off. I wasn't going to let anyone make it look worse than it was. A few cuts on a solider just added character was what I told myself as I refused to wince. Stepping through the doors and into the quiet of the library, a familiar smell of books made me feel somehow at home, but my attention was drawn to the flashing lights outside as a squad car pulled to a stop.

Two uniformed cops, both men, were fast to exit the car and head to the doors, coming through them just behind me. They both slid to a stop as they recognised me and I recognised them - they were the two uniforms with DS Spencer last night at the hospital and I could only imagine how pleased he would be to hear that I was involved in yet another incident now.

'Miss Aaronson,' the one on the left said, which caused several sets of eyebrows to raise.

I jumped in quickly to explain, speaking to Professor Grayhawk but loud enough that all those around me could hear. 'I was attacked last night and these gentlemen,' I indicated the cops, 'were there to investigate.'

Mercifully, neither of them argued, but I noticed the one who hadn't spoken yet leaned down to his lapel microphone as he went back out the doors.

What I said hadn't gone unnoticed though. Professor Holliman sounded shocked when he said, 'Two attacks in less than a day? Are you in some kind of trouble? Who were those men?'

He had already asked that question and my answer wasn't different the second time around. 'I have no idea. I don't know why that man attacked me just now, but it was a different set of circumstances last night and completely unrelated to today. Last night, I interrupted someone else being attacked and in so doing got myself involved. Whatever caused the man outside to attack me, I think he might have killed me if it were not for the second man's shield.'

I got blank expressions from everyone. 'What shield?' asked Professor Holliman.

Looking at the sea of confused faces, I could tell they hadn't seen it but some of them had to have been looking out of the window when he appeared. The faces were at the window right after I flung the man in the cowl at the glass. Now questioning my own sanity, I prompted them, 'Big, circular blue thing. Kind of see-through and had weird symbols all over it.' My audience exchanged questioning glances. 'No one saw that, huh?' I didn't know what that meant but I chose to downplay it. Smiling, I rubbed my skull, 'I guess I hit my head harder than I thought.'

My playacting diluted the concerned expressions but didn't kill them off completely. It did, however, convince a few of those watching at the periphery to peel off and return to whatever they were doing beforehand.

The policeman spoke to Professor Holliman, 'Is there somewhere private we can go? I need to speak with Miss Aaronson and any other witnesses.'

'Yes. Yes, of course, come right this way, please.' He started to move away and spoke to Delores as he walked backwards away from her, 'Can you get some tea? Or whatever Miss Aaronson would like. Right this way,' he repeated as he strode across the library.

To Delores, I said, 'Tea sounds great, actually. Thank you.' Then I followed Professor Holliman, the cop waiting for me to move so he could follow me. Did he really think I was going to run in the opposite direction?

I intended only to pop in so I could introduce myself, now it looked like I was going to be stuck here for hours. There was nothing desperate that I needed to do, but had planned to unbox my life and settle in to Sarah's flat and then see if I couldn't do some more research into the soul suckers, which I now believed were actually called shilt. However, I had new things to research now, maybe starting by asking the internet what was suddenly so interesting about me. I paused briefly as we crossed the library, my train of thought straying to the man with the surfer hair; he hadn't been either of the men today which gave me three interested men (I should be so lucky), some magic, and a race of things called the shilt.

The cop almost bumped into me as my feet stopped moving. 'Keep going, please, Miss Aaronson. I need to ask you a few questions and take a statement about this afternoon's attack.'

I heard his words and started walking again but my mind was whirling now. I felt like Alice down a rabbit hole. Or was it through the looking glass? I read them both as a child but couldn't pick one story from the other now. It didn't matter, I had returned from Zannaria and everything about the world had changed. Magic was real and I wasn't the only one able to do it. Furthermore, there were murderous creatures who, like vampires, sucked the life out of people, and they could vanish through a conjured portal. They weren't human but they could speak my language. The Cowl, I gave him a name too, was after me but didn't feel a need to explain his actions before attacking, and I got saved by a man with a shield that only I could see. I carried on listing all the weird shit until we reached a door on the far side of the library.

I needed to get this interview done quickly, excuse myself from my new colleagues, and find somewhere quiet to be so I could find out what the hell was going on.

Little did I know that my own display of magic had not gone unseen.

Chapter 10

As clandestine organisations go, the Supernatural Investigation Alliance was right up there. There were a few rumours to be found on the internet, but no one really knew anything about them. In public they operated as the Special Investigation Bureau, supposedly a branch of the police though they were nothing of the sort. The name was different in other languages, of course. Set up to address what was recognised as a growing supernatural problem, global governments were diverting funds to their activities at a staggering rate. Some of the funding was diverted to ensuring they stayed secret, snuffing out websites and conspiracy nuts who managed to stumble onto the truth. There was a global team run by the Americans just to suppress the press. The world population couldn't know the truth.

The headquarters of the British Division of the Supernatural Investigation Alliance was in an underground facility purpose-built for them during the enormous multi-billion-pound Crossrail project that ran east to west beneath London. It could be accessed on foot via an elevator inside an unmarked office inside a large office block in Canary Wharf. It was also connected by tube on a secret line with direct access to Westminster. It was far enough below ground that supernatural creatures such as shilt could not open a portal directly inside; power from the ley lines petered out more than ten yards above the highest levels.

Commissioner Michael Swinton felt safe in what was essentially an underground bunker, but he didn't feel in control. He might have tactical command for the UK, but the supernatural problem just wasn't understood, by him or anyone else. They were largely at the mercy of the few human supernaturals the SIA had employed, though employed was the wrong word for many of them. Take Otto Schneider, who had arrived at the HQ a few minutes ago and was demanding an audience right now. Schneider came and went as he pleased and was too powerful for them to do anything about. He was on their side, or so it seemed, so Swinton had to tolerate being summoned. He had two shifters on his payroll who were far easier to manage but also less effective and his bosses believed individuals like Schneider were the key to winning the war everyone believed was coming.

Secretly, Swinton had serious doubts about whether they were being misled. Yes, supernatural occurrences, which had been monitored for decades unbeknownst by the public, were on a meteoric rise, but did that mean they were heading for the cataclysm Schneider assured them might happen at any moment? Swinton would listen to what Schneider had to say today but then make up his own mind on how he deployed his forces.

The elevator took him up two levels to where the wizard would be waiting for him in a debriefing room. Met as the elevator doors opened by a junior intelligence operative, he saw Schneider lurking impatiently by a water cooler.

'He refused to go into the briefing room, sir,' advised his bespectacled junior in an apologetic tone. Even though the wizard could not draw on his magic at this depth, he still acted as if he was able to do as he wished.

Swinton couldn't remember the young man's name, but mumbled, 'Thank you, I'll take it from here,' as he crossed the room. Fixing his face so he wore a professionally courteous smile, he offered his hand to shake. It was not his first time meeting the young wizard but he hadn't spoken to him one to one until now. 'Herr Schneider, I assume you are here for an urgent matter?'

Otto noted the man had a firm handshake, not that he expected anything less. 'You need to deploy a quick reaction team to Rochester.' He made it a statement not a request. He couldn't give the man an order which was a shame but he wasn't about to take up a senior position within the Alliance just so he could influence decisions, he needed to be free to move.

Swinton frowned slightly, his brow creasing as he let the instruction settle. He wanted to bark a response but recognised the need for restraint. 'You are referring to the minor shilt incursion there last night?'

'No,' Otto shook his head. 'That might be inconsequential. I haven't determined why the shilt were there yet though it was possibly just random predation. There is something else going on and Sean McGuire was there. He attacked a woman in broad daylight which means he was there without any form of backup. That is outside of his usual method of operating so there must be a reason for it. Something is going to happen in Rochester, and you will want men there ready to react when it does. I know how keen you all are to keep your secrets.'

'Something is going to happen in Rochester,' Swinton repeated, keeping his voice neutral. 'Can you elaborate?'

Otto shook his head again, refilling his cup of water from the cooler as he answered, 'Not at this time. I intend to find out who the woman is. She might be of no consequence; she wasn't drawing ley line energy and she showed no signs of shifting so I don't know why Sean would have an interest in her.'

'Could it be a case of mistaken identity?'

Conceding the point though he thought it unlikely, Otto shrugged. 'I expect to know soon enough but expect trouble in Rochester or the surrounding region. I'm heading back there when I leave here.' Switching subjects, Otto asked, 'How many of the British familiars have you been able to contact?'

Swinton expected this very question and had an answer prepared. 'I have a team working on it.'

Otto called him on his bullshit, 'That is not an answer.'

Swinton narrowed his eyes; there was only so much arrogance he was prepared to take from the younger man. However, this wasn't his first command and he learned to defend his actions a long time ago. 'Results with such a complex task will be achieved in time. My operatives ...'

'You don't have time, Commissioner,' argued Otto, interrupting rudely. 'They are vulnerable, avoiding tapping a ley line because they know it will expose them, they need to be brought to a safe facility. Many of them are over a century old. Light bulbs were a new invention, cars hadn't been dreamt of. This is like an alien world to them.'

'Perhaps you should have considered that before you sent them all back here.' Swinton's retort was a red rag to a bull. Otto had risked everything to rescue hundreds of familiars trapped in the immortal realm and success came at great personal cost. It hadn't gone to plan, though, the resulting chaos saw the rescued slaves cast back into the mortal realm and no one knew where they were. Now he was trying to track them down, but Sean McGuire was doing the same thing and kept beating him to it – Otto was one, and Sean had an army of shilt plus other familiars still loyal to their masters on his side. Otto needed the SIA to help; they had divisions in every country.

Otto put his cup down and pulled a flame into his hand. Swinton's eyes flared and he took an involuntary step backward to get away from the flame. 'You forget yourself, Commissioner. I am a dangerous, immortal wizard who chooses to work with you. The familiars are your number one priority, am I clear about that?'

'How? How?' Swinton stuttered before getting himself back under control. The wizard had conjured flame when there was no ley line energy to be had. 'How can you do that this far below ground?' he demanded to know.

Otto closed his fingers to douse the fire. 'It's magic.' He drained his cup of water and dropped it into the recycle bin. 'Get the familiars, commissioner, and deploy a team to Rochester today.' Otto was already heading for the elevator; the conversation was over so far as he was concerned. If the commissioner chose to ignore him, he didn't care. Letting Rochester play out in front of the public might shortcut the route to the population discovering the truth.

The commissioner was following him as he got into the elevator, angrily shouting, 'You don't give orders here, Schneider.'

'Somebody ought to.' Otto's final insult was a harsh one he knew but perhaps it would get the man off his butt and moving. Three of the people he saved from the immortal realm had been killed this week. Sean was too powerful for them to stop and Otto doubted they even saw his attacks coming.

As the car ascended, Otto felt the ley line energy return, flooding into his body to rejuvenate him. The trick with the flame was about all he could do below ground; tiny particles existed in the air which could be used to power the simplest of spells. The Commissioner didn't know about it, clearly, and Otto liked to make sure he knew things that others didn't. Right now, the thing he didn't know was whether the woman had been Sean's real target or not. It was time to find out if there was anything interesting about her.

Chapter 11

I gave a statement to Constable Townsend, who introduced himself once we were sitting down. He was actually quite nice and spoke to me as if I were the victim and not the criminal, something DS Spencer hadn't managed in our two previous meetings. His colleague, and several others who arrived shortly after we adjourned to the side room, were interviewing other witnesses and it was clear that I had been ambushed by the man in the cowl. No one had seen anything much which worked in my favour as I tried to be lenient with the truth. I told PC Townsend the man had hit me and that was how I came to arrive on the ground with cuts and scratches; I didn't think saying he hit me with an invisible wall of air would help. The point is I didn't lie; I just didn't give him the whole truth.

My attacker was not known to me, and I couldn't give PC Townsend a facial description because all I had seen was his lips and chin, but I did my best to describe his clothing, shape, and height. PC Townsend had heard about the second man who came to my rescue from the general chatter, but I couldn't tell him much about that man either. Then he asked about the blinding flashes that witnesses reported. I watched them form above Cowl's head and I believed I had seen him create lightning in front of my eyes. I didn't say that though. I told him I was too busy cowering in fear to know what he had done or where the flashes came from.

When his radio squawked to get his attention, he reached up with his left hand to squeeze the button and leaned down to speak into it, 'Receiving.'

'You're requested at the main entrance.'

'On my way,' he replied and let the microphone go again. Then he pushed back his chair, downed the rest of his tea and stood up. 'That's probably DS Spencer. He'll want to read your statement before he comes in to speak with you himself.'

'He doesn't seem to like me very much.'

I got a half grin in response. 'Spencer doesn't like anyone very much. He's a good detective though. I'll be back in a minute.'

I nodded silently and the moment he shut the door, I was out of my seat and across at the window. I had endured enough of DS Spencer's nonsense and had no stomach for more. Also, I knew I couldn't tell him the truth, he knew I was lying every time I did it and no matter what I told him, I was quite certain the police could not protect me if Cowl returned. All in all, I felt I had good reason to go out the window. So that was what I did. I left behind my bag of clothes. It was just leggings, a hoody, and yesterday's knickers. I could come back for them another day or not at all; it really didn't matter in the context of the week I was having. I needed answers and I wasn't going to get any of them while in DS Spencer's company.

The window opened onto a car dealership. It wasn't much of a view for the professor to have from his office, but the library looked two hundred years old so maybe when they built it there was forest outside. I dropped about five feet into a two-footed landing and walked away as if I was supposed to be there. Passing between cars, I spotted a double decker bus about to pull up at a bus stop, so I jogged to it and swung myself on board just as the last passenger paid the driver their fare.

It was even going the right way, passing right by the library as I hid myself by sitting next to a much taller person - that's not hard to do when you are five feet tall. Ten minutes later, I was getting off and walking across the street to Sarah's flat.

Sarah had picked up my message when she woke up in the morning and sent a reply to let me know she was glad I wasn't dead. She also told me she scored with Ian and was seeing him again tonight. I think the subtext was that she might need to ask me to be out of the flat at some point in the near future, but I couldn't help wonder, even though I only saw them interact for a few minutes, if she managed to get somewhere with him because he was a bit drunk. I didn't put any of that in my reply though. She ended the message by telling me there was a key with the old lady next door, telling me her name was Rose and I should be prepared to smell cat pee when she opened the door.

She wasn't wrong.

'Hello,' I said, trying to keep the scarred portion of my face hidden under my hair as much as I could. I gave the grey-haired old lady my best smile as she peered around the door through the crack permitted by the chain. 'I'm Anastasia, Sarah's new flat mate next door.'

'Oh, yes. She said you might be calling around. Something about getting into bother last night and not having a key.' She walked away from the door, still nattering on as she disappeared into her flat. The chain stayed on, but I could hear what she was saying. 'You girls have it all these days, you know. I couldn't get up to the shenanigans you all do now. Back then, you were running the distinct risk of getting pregnant, Nowadays, you don't even need a pill, they can just stick a thing in your arm and hey presto; no babies.' She appeared back at the door, half of her face peering through the gap at me. 'Not that I blame you one bit. If I could do it all again, I wouldn't have married my Reggie. He was a terrible shag I don't mind telling you.'

'No, that's not ...' I tried to explain that I wasn't out with a boy but getting in a word edgeways wasn't going to happen and she still hadn't shown me the key. 'I would have had a lot more sex and then picked someone who was half-good at it. Still, nevermind. Nothing I can do about it now.' She held up the key, poking it through the gap. 'Here you go, love. Just you watch out for that aids thing, love. Never had to worry about that in my day. Herpes maybe, but nothing that was going to kill you.'

I gave up trying to burst her bubble, thanked her for the key, and escaped the first chance I got. She muttered something I didn't hear as her door closed and I opened Sarah's. I was inside and I was safe, or some false version of safe that four walls fooled me with. I couldn't hang around, DS Spencer was bound to send a car to look for me here; I gave him the address last night. Also, unless it was blind luck, Cowl had known to look for me at the library so could just as easily have this address too.

My big box of belongings was in my bedroom exactly as Sarah said it was. The room was small, barely ten feet long by maybe nine feet across and had a cheap, build-your-own bed, wardrobe, and chest of drawers which had each seen better days. The furniture didn't leave a lot of room for anything else, but I needed some things, so I tore the box open and did a very quick unpack. A lot of it went on the bed to be sorted later but some went into drawers.

With the box empty, flattened and stuffed into a corner down the side of the wardrobe, I changed into my third outfit of the day, one that was not only a lot more me but one it was easier to move in. I have suits, hand-cut ones, in fact, because the army provides a tailoring budget and expects its officers to look good. I wore them only when required to do so though and lived in jeans and stretchy tops most of the time when I wasn't in uniform or sports gear. I paired tight jeans with a pair of lace-up suede boots I bought on a whim years ago and then never wore. I was betting they would secure my left foot in place and they did. After the shilt ... I was training myself to call them that now, had ripped my foot off last night, I didn't want it to happen again. Actually, what I wanted was to never see another shilt again as long as I lived but I doubted that was going to happen.

A white sleeveless stretchy cotton top and a red zip up hoody because I wanted to hide my face completed the look. With the hood up I looked like Eliot from ET – I just needed a bicycle with a basket but enough time had already passed so I pushed idle musings to one side, grabbed my backpack from the side in the kitchen where I guess Sarah put it and checked to make sure my things were still in it.

My phone had died, and the charger was in the bag, so I needed that, and I wanted my laptop. Everything else I ditched onto my bed and was going to leave it until I spotted the candy bar and my stomach growled at me. I ripped it open as I went out the door. I would get something more substantial soon – I was going to lay low for the afternoon and see what I could work out for myself. Stage one of that was finding somewhere secluded where I could see just what I was able to do.

Chapter 12

From the bus I had seen that the land between the gaggle of flats where Sarah lived and the river half a mile away was woodland and a few fields. It was low lying and looked like it might be prone to flooding so I was going there in the hope I would find it deserted.

From her flat on Shorts Way, which was an elevated position looking down over the River Medway valley, I kept walking downhill until I ran out of houses. I had to look around a bit to find a passage that led between the houses to the land beyond and when I did, paw prints told me local dog owners brought their animals here daily for exercise. I would have to make sure there were none anywhere near me when I started throwing balls of energy around, but it was nearing mid-afternoon and I got lucky.

Finding a small clearing in the trees well off the trodden paths, I placed my backpack on the ground and took off my hoody. It was warm enough that I didn't really need it anyway, wearing it was so people wouldn't stare when I got to town.

'Right, Anastasia,' I said to myself. 'What can you do?'

The first time had caught me by surprise, the energy forming by itself as a defensive measure it seemed. The second time, I had done it deliberately but also in panic and the third time, when I faced Cowl, I had been able to confidently push the feeling of power from inside my body outwards to create the orb in my right hand.

Alone, and with time to think about what I was doing, I closed my eyes and tried to visualise the energy inside my body. I could produce it, but I didn't know where it was coming from. However, as I pushed out with my senses, the sensation of power was flowing into me from the Earth beneath my feet. My eyes snapped open so I could look at the soil and grass beneath my boots. There was nothing to see. I lifted a foot, but there was no tendril of light blue energy flowing upwards into it, yet I could feel it.

It filled my body as if it were flowing through my blood. This had to be something to do with the piece of shrapnel in my head. I wasn't happy about it. I couldn't be. The injuries were bad enough, not that I would ever allow myself to wallow for long in self-pity, but whatever this was, it wasn't doing me any favours. I could make orbs of energy in my right hand and use them as a weapon. It had some juice on it too, but while it might be classed as a superpower, what had I actually gained?

I answered the question for myself: I can hear supernatural creatures. The voices arriving in my head were just as unwelcome but if there were creatures like the shilt preying on people, which there were, then maybe I could stop them. Maybe I had to. I didn't think the police could and if everyone else just sees the enchantment they wear, then maybe I was the only one who could tackle them.

Closing my eyes again, I drew energy inwards until I could feel it fizzing and sparking in the centre of me. Opening my right eye just a crack, I looked down at my chest to find tiny blue arcs flashing over my skin where my cleavage would be if my boobs were big enough to justify the word. I closed it again and tried to push the energy down to my left hand. I knew it wasn't there but didn't know if that would matter or not.

Though I could visualise the energy in my left hand, I couldn't get anything to actually happen. I tried with my right, an orb forming instantly. I opened my eyes and fired it at a tree. It slammed into the trunk, rocking the whole thing to startle birds from its branches and from those of all the trees nearby. Where the orb had hit was a serious scorch mark.

Carefully, I removed my prosthetic hand and tried once more to send an orb down my left side; maybe I could fire it from the stump. I got the same result though. I put my left hand back on, making sure it fit snugly then tried my legs, curious to see if I could shoot blue energy from my right foot and found a handy rock to sit on so I could take my boot and sock off. I needn't have worried about blasting a hole in my boot though, just like my left hand, nothing happened. I could use my right hand and that was it.

I wanted to see what else I could do. Having seen Cowl produce lightning and hit me with an invisible wall earlier, I wondered if I could do that too. Also, the man who came to my rescue had a shield. I waved my arms around like I had seen Cowl do but I just felt silly. If there was a way for me to do those things, I couldn't yet work out how. Maybe if the shield guy turned up again, I would ask him.

Time was ticking on and I was getting hungrier, so I spent a few more minutes practising the blue orbs of energy, firing blast after blast at the tree with the scorch mark until I saw it begin to topple. I had been shooting at the same spot, forming the orb and then pushing my hand out like I was telling someone to stop. After a while, the tree started to smoke so I hadn't been able to see that I was blasting my way through it.

As the smoke began to clear, the poor tree fell lazily to one side, still attached by a few pieces of wood, but more than ninety percent severed.

I pulled an oops face, grabbed my bag and hurried away.

I must have been out of range of a phone tower because a hundred yards from where I had been, my phone suddenly started pinging. I had eight missed calls from an unknown number and two from Sarah. Sarah had also sent me a text message.

Ana, Mrs Tyler just called me to say the police were at the flat looking for you. Are you in some kind of trouble? Is this to do with last night? Because I don't need any hassle in my life right now. You haven't unboxed your things yet, so I think you should probably just find somewhere else to stay.

Okay, so that was a problem. I had given her rent money and we both signed a six-month contract so I was fairly sure I could be a dick about it and just refuse to move out. I doubted that would be a good policy in the long run, but I felt a little aggrieved because I hadn't done anything wrong. It was something I would have to deal with later when weird, magic-wielding men wearing cowls weren't trying to kill me.

Abicat22@gmail.co.uk because it had the heading: I saw you.

My stomach tightened as fear flooded my body. I clicked it with my right thumb to read the whole message, telling myself it might be nothing.

It wasn't nothing.

Hi, Anastasia,

This is Abi. I work at the library. I was outside when 'the incident' happened earlier and I saw what you did with your hand. We need to talk really soon.

Abi

I read it three times, gritting my teeth and muttering obscenities to the sky. When no one said anything, I figured no one had seen and allowed myself to relax. I was freaked out enough about all that was happening; I didn't need someone trying to blackmail me as well, since that was the obvious subtext of the message.

I paused with my thumbs hovering over the screen. When I worked out what I wanted to write in my reply, I sent:

Abi,

Where do you want to meet?

It was short and it asked the only pertinent question. I thought about playing dumb and insisting that I had no idea what she was talking about. I still might choose that option but I first I needed to know if she had any footage.

Almost instantly, an answer pinged back.

Are you still in Rochester?

If she wanted to blackmail me, it wasn't going to work. She would have to expose the truth and to hell with it. Not only did I not have any money, I was aware enough to know that blackmailers never stop once they start winning.

I sent back: *Yes.*

A few seconds later I got back instructions on where to meet her. She generously told me I could get there whenever, which gave me license to put it off to my eightieth birthday. I didn't do that though, I had fire in my belly and Abi was about to find out what I was made of. She was a snake who wanted to blackmail me and believed she had a small furry creature cornered. Well, today the small furry creature would turn out to be a mongoose.

Chapter 13

I thought it ironic that the place she wanted to meet was one of the very few places I could find my way to; I was going back to Eddy's Tavern at the bridge end of the High Street. The sky darkened as I got near, mirroring my mood as a bank of dark clouds moved in from the estuary where it met the English Channel. It threatened rain but I got to my destination before it started to fall, seeing umbrellas go up outside while I paused just inside the door and scanned around the almost empty room.

There were a few tables with people sat at them but none with a lone woman. Anton was behind the bar again, putting glasses away when I walked in. He called, 'Be right with you,' as an automatic reaction then saw who it was and, I guess, remembered me from last night.

I had my hoody back on, of course, so maybe he just remembered the tiny woman who hid her face. Either way, he was professionally polite and showed just the right amount of interest, asking me, 'Keeping okay?' while he poured my pint. He wasn't prying, he was giving me the chance to talk if I wanted to.

I offered him a smile, pushing my hood back a little so he could see my eyes before pulling it forward again to hide myself. 'I have nothing to complain about.' I got a raised eyebrow as if he was expecting me to offload my woes on him. It was time for me to be philosophical. 'We all have to expect a little rain in our lives. The sun cannot shine every day.'

He placed my pint on the bar, a small amount of foam running down one side as the head spilled over and I got a nod of approval for my opinion. 'Were you army?' he asked.

I couldn't blame him for his curiosity. 'I still am actually. I am waiting for my discharge. I'm not much use anymore.'

'I'm sure that's not true,' he argued.

'I meant for the army. It's an opinion I will agree with. Front line troops have to be one hundred percent, or they slow the team down and endanger it. It was good while it lasted but I work at the library now.'

He made a surprised face, which I thought was aimed at my change in career, but actually he knew something I didn't. 'There are two of your colleagues sitting just over there.' He nodded with his head rather than rudely point. 'See the tall woman?'

It was the woman who came to my rescue earlier. Just as he drew my eyes in her direction, the tall woman must have got the feeling that we were looking at her because she chose that moment to turn around. In so doing, she revealed a smaller woman obscured by her girth and height: Abi.

It had to be her. I sucked the top off my pint of ale, refreshing my mouth and savouring the taste as I let a grimace form inside my hood. I was going to have to take her outside for this. I like Anton and he showed me respect so I wouldn't disrespect his place by starting a fight in it.

However, to my great surprise, the woman I assumed was Abi bounced out of her chair like her tail was made out of rubber, waved to me with great enthusiasm, and started in my direction. The tall woman came with her. They were both smiling emphatically.

I was guarded when I said, 'Hello,' and kept my posture open, ready to fight if it came to it.

The smaller woman's smile could not have been any wider. 'Hi, I'm Abigail,' she said, 'This is Alexandra,' she introduced her friend. 'People call us Abi and Alex.' Abi was about five feet and seven inches tall which to my mind made her about average height for a woman. I would kill to be her height. She had dazzling black hair that reflected different colours and almost seemed to glow. She was Chinese, I thought, but might have been from Taiwan or somewhere close by. Her hair hung completely straight but curled under at the last inch where it just about touched her shoulders. It framed her face perfectly. She wore Ralph Lauren spectacles and carried a Karen Millen handbag that matched her coat. She had more money and style than me for sure. Her tall friend Alexandra had to be at least six foot two. In contrast to Abi, who wore three-inch heels, Alex chose flat ballet shoes, undoubtedly because she was already tall enough and very possibly because her foot size matched the rest of her, and she just couldn't get feminine shoes to fit. Her hair was brown like mine, a similar chestnut shade in fact and she had a long chin and a long nose and brown eyes the colour of mud.

They were both being far too friendly for women who planned to blackmail me. I decided to downplay my intended strategy. 'You invited me here, ladies. What can I do for you?' I hadn't put my hand out to shake. I hadn't introduced myself though they already knew my name and my question betrayed how guarded I felt I needed to be. The ladies looked confused, glancing at each other in question as if they had misunderstood something. I opted to be forward with them. 'Your email made it sound like you wish to blackmail me. Is that the case?'

Abi gasped and her hands flew to her mouth. 'Oh, my God! Of course not. Why ever would you think that?'

A wave of relief washed through me. 'Because that was the subtext of your message.' Horrified, Abi rushed back to their table to retrieve her phone and see what she had written, and I let my shoulders sag. 'Or that's how I took it.' I admitted. 'It might just be that I am a little paranoid.'

Abi's eyes danced across the tiny screen of her phone and she pulled an embarrassed face. 'No, I can see what you are saying. I'm really sorry.'

'No, I'm sorry. Look, I think maybe we should start again.' I pushed my hood back a little so they could see my eyes. 'I'm Anastasia. I'm very pleased to meet you.'

Alex said, 'Come and join us. We really want to talk to you.'

Remembering myself, I replied, 'I need to thank you for coming to my rescue earlier outside the library. I think you saved my life. It was a very heroic thing to do.'

Her cheeks flushed. 'Actually, I thought he was attacking a child,' she admitted. 'I'm not trying to insult you,' she looked down and indicated her own body. 'People call me Big Bird. It wasn't until after I hit him that I saw he was attacking a woman.' Then, because Abigail was still hovering a few feet away by the table, she started that way, beckoning with her right hand that I should join them.

I grabbed my pint, remembered that I was hungry and said, 'Just give me a second.' Anton saw that I was looking to get his attention, so when he came over, I ordered a burger and fries.

The girls were sitting opposite each other at a small round table with four chairs. I sat with Alex to my left, closest to the bar, and Abi to my right. The moment I sat down, Abigail leaned forward to speak quietly. 'So how did you make the energy blast thing? Are you a supernatural?' I could not have been more surprised if she had unzipped her head and taken it off to reveal a small person inside operating her like a marionette. Seeing my expression, she said, 'I saw it. I have been reading about this sort of thing on the internet for years. Don't worry, there's lots of you around.'

My mouth was hanging open, I was that shocked.

'Most people don't believe it,' added Alexandra, 'But Abi and I have been reading forums where people talk about their experiences and their stories are always the same.'

'Well, more or less,' Abi corrected her. Then she looked at me. 'Some people report having a relative kidnapped and dragged through a strange pool of shimmering air that then vanishes once the person has gone through it. Others report seeing creatures that most of the conspiracy nuts are calling aliens.'

'We don't think they are though,' added Alex.

'No,' agreed Abi. 'Popular theory is that this is all linked and there is an organisation covering it up and keeping it quiet. I've read reports of beings forming energy balls that they fired from the palm of their hands.' I glanced guiltily down at my own right hand. 'I couldn't imagine quite what that would look like until today when you did it.'

I wanted to laugh at their daft conspiracy theories and probably would have two days ago. Now I was part of the conspiracy. What I had heard though, was that these women knew a heck of a lot more about what was going on than me.

'Go on then,' prompted Abigail. 'What are you? A shifter? A witch? An Elf? I read in one forum that elf magic is the most powerful.' Abi either knew a lot and would have all the answers I needed or knew nothing at all and was just regurgitating things she had read which might be utter rubbish.

They had my attention though and they knew my secret. I could make out like they had imagined it, but I wanted their help to find out more about myself, the shilt and all the other weirdness going on around me.

I took a draught from my pint and savoured the taste, then set it back on the table and started talking. 'I don't know what I am.' It was an honest statement. 'I got injured in Zannaria,'

'What were you doing in Zannaria?' Alex asked.

'I was a soldier. I still am, I guess, but,' I paused to take my left hand out of my pocket where it had been since I walked in. Both women gasped when they saw the carbon fibre digits protruding from my sleeve.'

Alex had a hand to her mouth. 'I saw that earlier, but I thought you just had a bandage on or something. I didn't see what it was. You lost that out there?'

'That and my left foot.'

'Oh, God.' Abi shook her head in horror.

Then I reached up with my right hand to pull back the hood and show them my face. I had to turn slightly so that Abigail could see my scar. They probably saw it or caught sight of it earlier but now they were getting the full show. Both looked horrified. I shrugged. 'I won't be entering any beauty pageants, but I got out alive and others didn't.' I took another mouthful of my ale to fill the lull in conversation. Neither woman had said anything, so before they could come up with anything sympathetic to say, I got going again. 'Anyway, I don't know what I am, and I don't know what happened today, but the man who attacked me did so deliberately. I am his target. He knows who I am and came to the library looking for me.'

'Do you know who he is?' asked Abi. 'Or, you know, what he is?'

I shook my head. 'I haven't a clue. Until last night when all the weird stuff started happening, I had no idea I was even different. That was when I made the energy ball thing for the first time. And I could hear voices.' They both eyed me critically because it was the traditional claim of a crazy person. 'I was in here last night. First time ever, I only arrived in Rochester an hour before that.' I stopped talking because I was jabbering to them with unnecessary information. 'I heard a voice, it was unpleasant and rasping and it sounded hungry, like a predator stalking prey. And ... and I could feel where it was coming from, so I went to look for it.' I told them about the encounter with the two shilt and described them in as much detail as possible.

Abi pulled a small laptop from her bag and set it on the table. 'That sounds just like the creatures discussed in a group I follow on social media.' She clicked a few keys and turned it around so Alex and I could see. Then she scooched her chair around so we would all be on the same side, but it was awkward at the round table. Since the pub was still mostly empty, we moved to a booth with a socket which meant I got to charge my phone at least. All three of us pressed in close along one side with the laptop set in front of us. Just then Anton brought my food across, so I munched on fries as I looked at the page.

'The Realm of False Gods,' I read the title of the group. 'Why do they call it that?'

Abi answered. 'There are people on here who claim they were taken through that air portal thing and then found themselves in a different version of Earth.'

'Like a parallel universe?' I asked, pulling a disbelieving face.

'I guess,' she replied. 'Something like that.' Then she scrolled to find a thread she wanted to show me. It started with a post by a man who claimed his grandfather had returned after being missing for forty-seven years. That was strange enough but then said his grandfather hadn't aged at all in the intervening period. He had been enslaved in what he referred to as the immortal realm. His story wasn't the only one like that. There were a few stories about the shilt, though no one called them that. No one seemed to know what to call them but from the descriptions they were the same thing I faced last night. More regular, though, were stories where the person was reporting a death in the family and the victim was left with an odd mark on their neck and no known cause of death.

'Have you noticed it yet?' asked Alex. I gave her a questioning look.

Abi let me know what Alex was asking. 'All the threads suddenly stop. The newest one is months old and they all stopped at the same time.'

'Someone is getting to the people and shutting them up,' Alex explained. 'At least, that's what I think. That is why we said earlier about the organisation covering it up. There is a popular theory on all the forums that spring up that a government organisation is suppressing information.'

I didn't know what to make of that. Abi took me to another website, one on which a single reporter had collated newspaper reports. 'This one is still live,' she told me.

The journalist listed incidents stretching back more than thirty years. He believed they were the work of wizards and had clearly done a lot of research. Each incident was referenced with a link so we could jump to it and be content he wasn't making it up. It made for compelling reading though I had to admit that each event could be written off as either a hoax or a stunt or just plain misconstrued. However, when Alex clicked a link to an event in Germany, my heart stopped beating.

Both women saw me tense up. I had a French fry hanging half out of my mouth. It was the man from earlier, the one with the shield.

'Who is that?' I stammered. 'That's who protected me with his shield.'

'What shield?' Both Alex and Abi asked at the same time.

Now I had to go for it; these two were in the inner circle already after all. 'Just before the man with the long coat and the hood ran off, he created lightning to use against me. Or it was something like that,' I corrected myself, acknowledging that I didn't really know what it was. 'Then this guy shows up just as the hooded man is launching it at me and shoves a shield in the way. You were closest. Did you really not see it? It was like a big disc of blue glass about two yards across.'

Both shook their heads, confounding me again. I hadn't imagined it. I hadn't. Pushing it to one side, I leaned across to get as close to the screen as I could. The three of us were crammed along the bench chair on one side of a booth with Alex in the middle and me on the outside.

'I need a name,' I begged. But the report didn't give one. The photograph had been taken at night in January 2012, and showed the man running away. Much like today when I saw his face, he was glancing back over his shoulder when the photographer caught him. The journalist believed the man was a wizard and responsible for many deaths in Bremen.

Abi announced that she needed another drink. Alex offered to get them but as I slid out to let her get to the bar, a question occurred to me. 'How come you two were in the bar in the middle of the afternoon. Do you work part time?'

Abi made an embarrassed face. 'Alex and I were so excited about seeing you do the energy ball thing that we skived off. Actually, Alex played up the bump to her head and said she felt woozy and I told them I felt traumatised by the attack. Professor Holliman folded like wet tissue.' She grinned at me. 'Honestly, if you ever want a day off, the merest suggestion that you have your period and he'll run a mile.'

Alex returned with fresh drinks for her and Abi and a bottle of sparkling water for me. Another pint of the delicious pale ale appealed but staying sharp and focused sounded a better plan since I had no idea when the man in the cowl might reappear. Thinking that made me worry. What if he turned up here? There were lots of people around and the lightning thing looked likely to hurt. I didn't want innocents to get injured just because I felt safer in public.

A plan began to form in my head as I considered my predicament. Cowl might never return, or he might walk through the door in the next minute, but I wasn't of a mind to sit around waiting to be attacked. I was going to go on the offensive.

We had been chatting and reading articles online for almost two hours and the pub was beginning to fill with people coming in for a drink on their way home from work. The noise increased but that didn't distract us.

When the topic of conversation swung back to the creatures I killed last night, both in Rochester and at the hospital, I explained what I knew about the shilt, which wasn't much to be fair. Alex asked, 'Should we go to the police. There was a detective at the library today who was very keen to speak with you. He seemed quite disappointed you were not there. Maybe we should track him down.'

I shook my head with a weary smile. 'That's Detective Sergeant Spencer. He thinks I'm the one responsible. A nurse was killed last night and lots of the children had those suck marks on their necks. DS Spencer thinks I know who the killer is.'

'Well, you do know who the killer is,' Alex pointed out.

She had me there.

Abigail jumped in. 'There's something I don't understand.' Alex and I turned to look at her. 'You said they look reptilian.'

'That's how I would describe them,' I agreed.

Abi nodded. 'Right, and you said there were lots of them. How do they not get spotted straight away?'

I thought I knew the answer to that one. 'I think they wear some kind of enchantment. One that makes them look ... I don't know, human maybe. When I faced the first two, they seemed very surprised I could see what they were.'

'You can see through their enchantment?' asked Abigail.

I thought about being able to see the shield when no one else could. 'I guess. Maybe that's another part of this ...' I mimed shooting a ball of energy from my hand. 'Whatever this is. I'm not like the two men today. I can't do the things they do. I think what I can do is coming from the piece of metal in my head.'

At six o'clock, Abigail announced she needed to go home. She was getting hungry and needed to feed her cats.

'Abi has cats,' Alex explained.

I got that from her statement about having to feed them and wasn't sure what Alex was trying to add. 'They are in tune with the mystical forces,' Abigail whispered as if it was a big secret. 'I really should go,' she said, getting up to force Alex and me out of the way so she could escape.

Alex got up too. 'I ought to get moving along. I have a date with a microwave meal to look forward to but if I have any more gin, I won't get up for work tomorrow and I'm not sure they will buy the traumatised excuse again.'

When I settled back into the booth, they both paused to look at me. 'You're waiting for something, aren't you?' asked Abigail.

Mostly I was waiting for dark.

Chapter 14

While we chatted this afternoon and the girls drank gin, I had been working out how I could turn things around. It was basic military strategy: do what the enemy is not expecting. Another great strategy is to hit them so hard and so constantly, and with such violence that they crawl back into their holes and never come out again. My first hurdle was not knowing where to find my enemy and that was why I had chosen to wait for dark.

I was guessing, if I am being honest, that the shilt would return once darkness fell. I had only seen them at night, not that two incidents could be called a trend. It was what I had to go on and my plan was to listen for their voices and then find them. I felt confident, after this afternoon's practice, that I could produce the energy balls at will. I would trap one of them and force it to tell me where Cowl was. And who he was. And, if I could beat it out of the unfortunate shilt, what Cowl's weaknesses are and how to beat him.

Another reason to wait for dark, was so I could sneak back to Sarah's flat. I would first need to call Sarah and try to reason with her about the flat and my innocence because I needed her to confirm there weren't still cops waiting outside in the street. I could speak with DS Spencer again another day. I really wasn't in the mood right now. If I thought he would listen to me and act on the information I had, I would be all over him, but I knew he wouldn't.

Abigail had asked if I was waiting for something and when I shrugged, rather than explain I was still avoiding the police, she sat back down. 'Are you waiting for dark so you can go hunting creatures like Buffy the Vampire Slayer? Because if you are, I'm coming with you.'

'Me too,' said Alex, bumping Abigail with her hip and sitting down too, all excited again at the prospect.

Doing my best to look innocent I lied to them. 'No ladies, I am just going to finish my drink and wander home. I'll see you in work tomorrow though, yes?' Now they look disappointed, the prospect of adventure denied just as swiftly as they imagined it. 'Hey, Alex, thanks again for earlier.'

I got a nod and a smile. 'You're welcome.' Then both women crossed the bar and went out the door. Alone in the booth, I closed my eyes and concentrated. The sun was setting but not down yet so listening for the voices of the shilt might be pointless. I didn't know for certain either way but a rap on the table made me jump.

I flinched back and felt myself automatically open the palm of my right hand as adrenalin pushed me into fight mode.

There were four middle-aged women in business attire holding glasses of wine. 'Can we have your booth?' one asked. 'Sorry, we don't mean to oust you, but you have space for six and it's just you.' She indicated around the bar, which now had very few available seats and no tables anywhere.

'We've been at a trade fair all day,' explained another of them. 'Our feet are killing us. You don't have to go; we could just join you.'

I stood up silently and left the booth, horrified that I had been just about to blast them. I was going to have to watch how I reacted. As I moved away, the women were muttering about me being rude because I hadn't said anything. I left them to it and found a corner by the door so I could wait.

Chapter 15

Sean hung in the air as the glowing white binding continued to slowly constrict around his arms and chest. He was a foot off the ground, no more, but helpless to change his situation as Daniel explained his displeasure.

'I felt I made the urgency of this situation clear to you.'

'You did, master,' Sean struggled to say, drawing in just enough air to make the reply.

Daniel peered up at the wizard, a flicker of annoyance passing over his face. 'And yet, a full day has passed, and you have nothing to show for it. Why is that?'

'I tracked her to a hospital.'

'Let's not overstate your abilities now, Sean,' Daniel chided his familiar. 'The shilt returned from the hospital with a tale of a woman who had attacked them with source energy. You knew exactly where to find her; no tracking was required.'

'Yes, master,' Sean squeaked. He gasped for breath, now unable to talk. Sighing, Daniel released him, the wizard tumbling to the ground and collapsing as he drew in ragged breaths to replenish his oxygen-starved body.

Sean knew he wouldn't be given much respite from the torture if he didn't start talking, so he went with unembellished truth this time. 'By the time I located her, she had already left, so I tracked her to her place of work, a library in Rochester, not far from the cathedral.'

'Ah, yes, the artefact. We shall return to that subject shortly. Please continue.'

Sean pushed himself off the ground, standing up though he didn't bother to straighten his clothes or brush off the dirt that now clung to his coat. 'At the library, I engaged her. She hit me with source energy, but I was able to subdue her.'

Daniel interrupted again, his anger making his fingers twitch as he considered hurting the wizard again just to make sure he stayed motivated, 'If you subdued her, why is she not now here with us?'

'Otto Schneider turned up. He came from nowhere and prevented me from taking her.'

Daniel's agitated movements stopped at the mention of his former familiar's name. Now he really was angry, and Sean flinched away as the demon glared at him. 'Did you not fight him?'

Sean was staring at Daniel's right hand, wondering what awful spell might come from it as he answered meekly, 'I fought, but I don't think he knew why I was there, and I chose to withdraw. If he learns what the woman is, he will surely protect her. I believed a better strategy was to return later with greater forces. Had I taken her then, I would still have needed to wait until nightfall to return here and risked further encounters with Schneider where I might have lost her. Perhaps, when I return, you will accompany me?'

Daniel narrowed his eyes but chose not to throw the incantus spell that would render his familiar immobile. 'I cannot accompany you. I am being watched too closely. My rivals here grow suspicious and jealous. That is why it is imperative that I get the girl and obtain the artefact.' He had to concede that a prolonged battle with Otto Schneider would have gained nothing, but he didn't voice his thoughts. He had expected Otto to interfere where he could and knew that he would target Sean because of his recent activities. It was an annoyance, but he expected Sean to overcome the hurdle in his way and complete the task. 'You will return as soon as we finish this conversation. I want that girl. Take all the shilt you need.'

'Yes, master.'

'What of the artefact? Did you locate it?'

Sean swallowed before answering, still worried that Daniel might yet punish him for failing to have all the answers. 'The marker is in the cathedral as you expected it would be. However, I wasn't yet able to confirm that the artefact is there.'

'Why not?' snapped Daniel, his voice loud like a thunderclap which again made Sean flinch.

'The second marker is on the ground, master. To confirm the artefact is there, I will have to dig up the floor of the cathedral. It would draw attention. I must do so stealthily or wait until I have the woman with me so it can be retrieved.'

The demon huffed out a breath through his nose. It would serve no purpose to rush and risk alerting the mortal population to what he believed lay beneath the floor of the ancient building. It was already in a place from which he could not retrieve it. The humans might move it, but he thought it more likely they would discover what it was and put it somewhere even harder to get to. That was if they didn't all die touching it.

'Very well, Sean. Use what resources you must but get me that woman.'

Daniel walked away, leaving Sean to finally take a deep breath and relax. Or relax as much as a wizard can when he is a demon's familiar. It was already dark where he would find his target, the sun having set a short while ago. He hadn't wanted to return to the immortal realm but when the shilt told him Daniel was waiting for an update, he knew he had no choice but to comply. Now he was going back to the mortal realm and this time he would get the woman no matter whether Otto Schneider turned up or not.

The shilt were already there waiting to spring a trap.

Chapter 16

My head snapped up when I heard the voice. It was different from last night, instead of sounding hungry and wanting to feed, it said my name. 'Anastasia,' it rasped, the voice even sounding like it was made by something inhuman.

Instantly I had a direction. The bar had offered a sense of company even though I steered away from making conversation with anyone after the girls left. It also supplied a room filled with potential victims if I got attacked there, so I left shortly after Abi and Alex and for the last thirty minutes I'd been walking slowly along Rochester High Street. To kill time, I looked at shops and businesses, poked my nose into alleyways when I saw them, just to see where they went, and did what my army instructors called understanding the battlefield. If I was here, then Cowl would come for me here. I hoped to find the shilt first and, as planned, beat some information out of them, but I couldn't control Cowl's movements, only my own.

When the voice called my name, I had been walking in the wrong direction. It turned me around and quickened my pace. It was back toward the bar but off to the left somewhere. Glancing up, I could see the two-story Elizabethan buildings above me, and beyond them the giant cathedral. The moon was bouncing light off the slate tiles of the cathedral's roof where a brief rain shower earlier had dampened it before moving on to let in clear skies.

At Northgate, the voice echoed in my head again, drawing me up toward the cathedral and the castle which lay beyond it. They were further on from that still, another hundred yards or more and not far from where I found the first two the previous night, I thought.

I felt no nerves. Even though this was all so new to me, I felt I could handle a couple of shilt without too much trouble. My plan was to sneak up on them. Until I worked out how their portal thing worked, I didn't want to run the risk of killing the first of them only to have the second vanish before I could stop it.

Passing the cathedral on my left and the castle on my right, I was going up a slight incline to a road called The Mews. I was less than one hundred yards from where I had found them last night, which might have been deliberate on their part since one of them was calling my name to draw me in. The soldier part of me was certain I was walking into an ambush and it made me pause. If I had a choice, I would draw them onto turf I had chosen myself and maybe even prepared.

I huffed with indecision, acknowledging that I didn't have the option I wanted. Cowl wasn't here at the moment. Or, at least, I wasn't currently being attacked by him which wasn't necessarily the same thing. For all I knew, he was hiding around the corner with the shilt, but either way I needed to get on and attack them, find out what I needed to know and ...

'What're you doing, Ana?'

I screamed and almost wet my knickers when a person spoke right next to my ear. It was most unsoldierly, but I had been caught completely by surprise. Collapsing against the wall as my heart restarted, I turned to find Alex and Abi behind me, Alex towering over me yet again to blot out the moon as I looked up.

'My, God, you almost gave me a heart attack. What is wrong with you two?' I snapped.

Abi was virtually vibrating with excitement, asking me a question instead of answering mine. 'Are you hunting? Are there supernatural beasts nearby that you are about to zap?' she asked, flicking her hand out like Spiderman shooting a web.

I didn't have time to answer because the shilt had heard my scream and, drawn by the thrill of a meal, were coming to attack. I heard them coming, my head filling with their excited chatter as I backed away and I instantly knew it wasn't two of them as I hoped. It was more like twenty. They weren't in sight yet, but they were coming.

'We have to go,' I murmured, turning around to shove the two women back toward the relative safety of the High Street where they could mingle in with other people. I could fight the shilt, but I didn't want to have to worry about Abi and Alex getting caught up in it.

'Who are these guys? Alex asked, pointing to a whole line of shilt coming out of an alleyway to cut off their route back to the town centre.

Quickly, I snapped out a question. 'Alex what do they look like to you?'

She shot me a curious look, glancing back at them and then back at me. 'What do you mean? They look like guys. A couple of them are quite cute. Especially that one,' she pointed to the third shilt in from the right, smiling at him as she did.

It confirmed my thoughts about the enchantment they used because I could see a dozen ugly, snake-like shilt in human clothes. 'Ladies, those *men* are not what you think. They are shilt disguised as men using a spell or charm or something.'

'Are you sure?' asked Alex, sounding disappointed. 'What about that cute one with the brown skin? He just winked at me.'

I rolled my eyes, but before I could retort the shilt started towards us as one body. I shoved back the sleeve of my hoody to expose my right hand and pushed sparking blue energy into it. It caused the line to pause, but a voice from behind us, coming to me via my ears this time, made the three of us spin around.

We *had* been ambushed, the first shilt to appear doing a great job of distracting us so the main force could get into position. At their centre was a creature twice the size of the shilt. It had to be over eight feet tall and twice as wide, its muscles were bulging and its features, while different, were equally gruesome. Tusks protruded from its lower mandible, distorting its lips, and its face was fuzzy with hair that looked more like fur, but also looked to have moss growing in it. Mentally, I labelled it as an ogre.

'Attack!' it bellowed, the volume alone enough to startle me into action.

Abi and Alex both squealed in fright as my own heart rate doubled from the jolt of adrenalin. It was fight or flight time, but with my new friends here, I was going to have to find a way to do both. The first blast from my right hand flew straight at the ogre, the time from leaving my hand to cross the twenty-yard distance about half a second. I expected it to take his head clean off, but it didn't. It didn't do anything because he raised a shield, demonstrating some ability to wield magic that was undoubtedly going to be a problem for me. My ball of energy hit it and dissipated with a flash of sparks.

'Ana!' yelled Alex. The two women were standing right by me. I had hold of Alex's coat with my left hand so she wouldn't stray; I couldn't fight the shilt and watch my new friends at the same time, but if the shilt now all had shields, I couldn't fight them at all.

Fast footsteps brought my attention around to see those with the ogre now running at us. There were too many for me to be able to hit them all even if they didn't have shields and there was another flank running at us from the other direction.

I made a decision based on the terror I felt and shouted, 'Run!' as I took off back toward the city centre. Our path was blocked, but this was better than waiting for them to converge on our position. We would either make it or we wouldn't. Mercifully, when I fired my next shot, it tore straight through the shilt I aimed at. I followed it with volley after volley to punch a hole through the advancing line. Each creature it hit, tried to deflect the blast with their knife or tried to duck, but I was too fast and when they did get their blades up, the blast went straight through them.

It wasn't possible to get them all but we ran at them as they ran at us which meant the ones to the furthest left and right escaped my hand cannon because they wouldn't be able to reach us before we were on the other side. Still holding Alex's coat, we passed through where the shilt had been, their bodies now disintegrating, and had all of those remaining behind us. Alex, her legs at least a foot longer than mine had got up to speed now and was outpacing me. So too was Abi, who had kicked off her heels to sprint across the cobbles barefoot.

There was no way I was going to slow down, but we were coming into a populated area with a platoon of shilt hot on our asses; I had to find a way to stop them. There was a little time yet, we were just coming up on the cathedral, but the moment we rounded the corner, I saw there were civilians there, tourists undoubtedly, taking photographs and doing touristy stuff.

I skidded to a stop as I turned myself around and started firing. Cries of alarm came from the people by the cathedral as the battle lit the air directly in front of them. My shots were ineffective as, yet again, the ogre used his shield to diffuse my blasts. The other shilt were behind him as they continued to advance, more slowly now, and my attention, which should have been on the enemy, was being distracted by screams of warning from Abi and Alex.

I didn't get to question why before a wall of invisible energy picked me up and slammed me into a wall. The pain as I cracked my skull against the ancient stone made me black out momentarily. I knew I needed to get my right hand up so I could fight, and my brain was screaming for me to find the new source of attack and do something to defend not only myself, but everyone else here.

Then I was yanked off the ground, hands going around my waist and just as my head moved, a shilt weapon, one of the short obsidian knives, struck the stone where my face had been not a second before. It had been thrown with the intention to kill, the thrower missing by the narrowest of margins, but an angry shout drew my eyes away from him and to the right where I saw Cowl.

'I need her alive!' he raged, turning his own attack against the shilt who had thrown the blade. Lightning flashed from above his head to kill the unarmed shilt. 'Anyone else throws their weapon and they get the same!' he roared. The shilt dropped to the ground but I noted that it didn't disintegrate the way they do when I shoot them.

I was being carried by Alex, one long arm around my middle, as she ran for all she was worth. My weight did nothing to slow her, but I couldn't return fire from this position, my right arm was pressed against her body as she took me ever closer to the busier part of the old city. I didn't want to go that way, there were too many innocents there.

'Alex, stop!' I shouted, though she either didn't hear me or didn't care because she continued onward, racing over the cobbles as the shilt chased behind. Not for long though. Another blast of air hit us, and this time I saw it coming, the air rippling as a pulse of it came after us like a swarm of invisible bees. I got just enough time for the words, 'Look out!' to appear on my lips, but no time to shout them, before the pulse wave picked us both up.

We tumbled arse over teakettle, blind luck providing a patch of grass to land on instead of the cobbles. Ahead of us, Abigail avoided the latest assault, cowering behind the solid stone of North Gate. If we could get to that, it might offer some respite, or a position from which I could hope to defend myself. Right now, we were exposed, and I knew there was no hope to get to the sanctuary any of the nearby structures offered.

The people had scattered, tourists and locals alike, seeing the fight and choosing to escape though there were a dozen faces peering around the corners as the cathedral plaza met the High Street.

Alex and I were jumbled together where we had fallen. My left arm was trapped beneath her body and my body was over the top of hers, which necessitated a forward roll on my part so she could sit up.

Alex groaned, 'Goodness, that was jolly unpleasant.' It was an understated response, but how was it that she even had time to make it? Why weren't they attacking now we were down?

Extricating myself from under her, I looked up to find Cowl crossing the cobbled street toward me. Behind him was the remaining shilt and their enormous leader. Cowl's approach was calm, as if he were walking to the bakers for a loaf of bread. 'I genuinely mean you no harm,' he said, his voice coming from somewhere deep inside the cowl itself.

'Oh, yeah? All the violence had me fooled!' I yelled back at him, pushing myself onto my feet even as he gestured for me to stay down.

Cowl stopped roughly three yards from me, thirty shilt a further three yards behind him in a gaggle with the ogre at the front. Cowl spoke again, 'My name is Sean McGuire. I apologise for attacking you earlier. At the time, I thought it the simplest approach. I see now that I should have chosen to speak with you instead.'

'What is it you want?' I asked. Alex was back on her feet and brushing dirt from her clothes, tutting at blobs of mud that might never come out. Since he wanted to talk, I saw no reason not get some answers.

'I wish to employ your skills.' I think he had more to say, but he was interrupted by two uniformed police arriving. They were both women, running around the side of North Gate while holding their heavy utility belts with one hand to stop them flapping around too much.

Alex punched the air, shouting, 'Jolly good, the fuzz are here. Now you're for it!' She pointed at Sean and the shilt beyond him. 'It's them you want, officers.'

Her help was completely unnecessary. Any fool could see the aggressive gang and their leader pinning the two women in place. I didn't like this though; it couldn't end well.

It took the cops about half a second to assess the scene, one jabbering into her mike and the other advancing. She didn't even get the chance to speak. Sean raised his right hand, a fast motion that produced yet another blast of air to bowl both women over. Screams and gasps of surprise came from the crowd of witnesses now trying to watch from the false safety the buildings supplied.

I wanted answers, but he had just attacked two cops and I wasn't okay with that. As his arm had been coming up to throw his spell, my own right arm was filling with the energy I could pull from inside myself. I heard Alex whoop, 'Get him, Ana!' just before I pushed the ball of energy from my palm and I knew it was going to hit him because he was looking at the cops still and not me.

The moment it left my hand, I pushed off with my good foot, giving Alex a shove to get her moving. We needed to get to a position I could defend. Nothing had gone to plan so far, I was outnumbered, the ogre had a shield that could defeat my only weapon, and the whole place was littered with civilians who were about to get caught in the cross fire.

Northgate was ten yards away, if we could get there, Alex and Abi could escape and usher everyone else to safety while I tried to hold the enemy at bay. That Sean wanted me in one piece was a big help to my plan, but no sooner had I started running than a figure fell out of the sky to land in front of me.

He blocked my escape route and he looked royally pissed.

Chapter 17

One second, I had a clear route to the North Gate, the next, it was filled with the man who came to my rescue earlier. That he had flown like superman to land in front of me brought a new set of questions I didn't have time to ask.

'Get out of the way,' he growled as his hands swirled. He was going to send a spell through me if I didn't get out of the way, that much was obvious. But I was running toward him and the danger he represented, my weight pitched forward so the best I could manage was to fall over at his feet as whatever he was cooking up left his right hand. I caught a close-up glimpse of his face as I fell; stubble on his face and crew cut hair, but the madness in his eyes was what stayed with me.

I bounced off the cobbles yet again, bruising my knees and ribs and jarring the stump of my left arm as the prosthetic hand hit the ground. Alex looked to fare little better as she fell the other side of the man. I didn't know who he was, or even his name but he was the one in the picture I saw this afternoon, no doubt about it whatsoever. The report said he was a mass murderer.

He stepped forward, menacing steps taking him toward Sean and the shilt. I could see the ogre's shield raise to defend himself, but when a rip of lighting tore into the earth near his feet, the sheer power of it still found a way to blast half a dozen shilt backwards.

'Damn you, Schneider!' screamed Sean. My blast had knocked him down and kicked him five yards to the side, but he was back up and readying his own spells.

Schneider, I labelled him in my head now that I had a name, flung more lightning in Sean's direction but it was caught in the sky by whatever Sean was doing where it changed direction and channelled directly into the earth.

I got back to my feet and launched my own attack. Now that Alex had scrambled away, I felt I had a free hand to wade in. The shilt were shifting to their right, moving to a flanking position that would draw Schneider's attention in two directions and give them an advantage they could press. I fired at them, blast after blast, but each was caught by the ogre's shield as if I were shooting foam balls from a toy gun. What had torn the shilt apart last night, was doing nothing now provided they stayed behind the ogre's protective barrier.

Schneider shot me a disgusted look and growled, 'Stop helping,' an obvious German accent making the familiar words sound strange.

I had no idea who he was and no reason to believe he was on my side. Saving me earlier might have been a mistake on his part. Either way, I wasn't taking any orders from him. There were still civilians watching the battle as they peered around the corners of North Gate and the fight raged ever closer to them.

An errant blast of flame from Sean's hand struck the awning above a small, and now very much emptied, brasserie and set it ablaze. Dancing light from it threw shadows across the tableau of the castle grounds as the shilt continued to advance. They were in front of the cathedral now and would soon be behind Schneider as he fought Sean. Apparently, that was what he had been waiting for. My ineffective shots continued to do nothing but as the shilt stepped onto the grass in front of the cathedral, Otto threw up his shield, protecting himself from Sean's next attack as he focused on his other flank. The shilt were ten yards from him but they didn't see the attack coming until it was too late.

Screaming sirens filled the air as cops bore down on us from multiple locations. They were less than a minute away I judged, but Schneider ended the fight, and the danger the shilt represented right then by burying them all. Whatever magic he used, it tore a huge divot of soil from the ground, ripping it out from under the shilts' feet as they walked over it. The ogre's shield faltered and suddenly, my energy blasts were able to get through. As they fell into the hole Schneider created to vanish from sight, I hit at least half a dozen of them, their bodies falling before I could see if they fell apart like before or not.

Sean tried the same on his opponent, the ground beneath my feet rumbling to give me a split second of warning. Panic shot through me, fear telling me to leap and run, but as the ground gave way, I began to fall backward out of control.

Schneider caught my left hand just as my feet went out from under me, pulling me into the sky as he rose above the street. He was flying again, but not for long. The next second, my body contorted in pain as the world and everything in it went white.

Randomly firing neurons told me I had just been hit with lightning, but I couldn't get my brain or body to work properly and now, instead of falling into a hole in the ground, I was falling from the sky. It wasn't exactly an improvement.

Mercifully, it turned out that Schneider hadn't taken me very high. My landing still hurt though; yet more scuffs and bruises to add to my list and the taste of blood in my mouth.

I could hear Sean laughing. 'The great Otto Schneider beaten by a mere mortal wizard.'

To my left, as I painfully rolled over to right myself, Otto Schneider was also getting back to his feet. 'You know I have to kill you, don't you, Sean?'

'I know that you will try,' Sean replied, circling warily to his left. The two wizards were no longer throwing spells, they were eyeing each other instead as they talked. 'You should not have given them false hope. The freedom you provided was a punishment not a blessing.'

'Only because you have tracked them down and killed them!' Schneider roared as he loosed a new spell, but Sean leapt backward into the air, deflecting Schneider's magic with his own.

'I will kill them all, Schneider. You cannot be everywhere.'

Calmly Otto sent another arc of lightning at his opponent, shouting over the sound of it, 'I don't have to be everywhere, you Irish arshloch. I just have to be where you are.'

The wailing police sirens were right on top of us now, not that I thought the police could do anything to stop these two men, but Sean took that as his cue to leave, propelling himself upward into the night sky with another ripple of air.

Schneider was going to go after him, my hand grabbing his arm the only thing that stopped him from blasting himself upward into the night sky. I was seriously bored with being in the dark. I needed to get some answers, so though I had no idea who Otto Schneider was or what side he might be on, he was the one who hadn't yet tried to kill me.

'Wait,' I begged him, making the word come out as if it were an order not a plea. 'Who are you?' I asked. 'Who did you set free that he is now killing?' All I had to go on were snippets of detail I picked up during the fight.

He yanked his arm free, pulling me off balance to stumble forward a step. The angry sneer on his face told me he wasn't going to give me any answers, but just before he took to the sky, he asked, 'What are you?'

Then he was gone, and the police were here.

Chapter 18

There had been no escaping the police this time. I was too beaten up to attempt to run away and the armed response unit that showed up looked hopped up enough that they might just shoot me anyway if I tried.

The hundred-yard expanse of ground between the cathedral and the castle looked like a battle zone and the police wanted answers. A whole chunk of it had been turned over when Otto buried the shilt and the ogre. I didn't know how far down they were, but it looked like quite a way. I could see sediment lines running through the soil where ancient rivers or an inland sea might have dumped them a million years ago. The shilt hadn't been seen since, I knew that much.

Four officers armed with Heckler and Koch assault rifles advanced on me, their rifles trained on my centre as if I was a threat. Okay, in theory I was, or, at least, could be a threat, but their nervous faces convinced me I would be shot dead the moment I started to push energy into my right hand, so I refrained from even thinking about doing so.

I didn't want to go to the police station, but I also knew I wasn't going to get any choice in the matter.

Obeying their barked orders to get on my knees, I complied, but not without protesting my innocence. 'Really? Do I look like the one causing all the mayhem?' I shook my head to make the hood fall back. It exposed my scar which gave them all pause when they saw it. The crowd at North Gate couldn't see it from their angle, which, given how many cameras were undoubtedly filming me, was a blessing.

Whether they thought I was the terrorist who had set the fire now raging over the Brasserie or not, they weren't taking any chances. With their guns effectively pinning me in place, two more cops came around behind me to push me roughly onto the ground. When one went to cuff me, he grabbed my prosthetic hand and jerked as he shouted, 'Weapon! I've got a weapon!'

With my chin held just above the cold cobble-stones, I snarled, 'That's my prosthetic arm, you idiot. Why don't you just rip it off for me? I'll bet that will be comfortable!'

'She's the victim!' I heard a woman shout. It might have been Alex, but I couldn't tell for sure with so much background noise. 'Police brutality! Police brutality!' the same voice cried, this time confirming that it was Alex.

The cop pulled back my sleeve to confirm that I did indeed have a prosthetic limb and their treatment of me altered for the better at that point. I still got cuffed, but I was cuffed by my right wrist to a female cop and they removed my left hand so I couldn't do anything with it. I tried to see it from their side, but it was a struggle.

A senior officer introduced himself as Superintendent Smith of the Specialist Firearms Command, SCO19. I was sitting next to the female police officer in the back of a police prisoner van when he found me. The female officer hadn't asked me any questions other than my name and whether I wanted a drink of water.

When he appeared, Superintendent Smith said, 'You can take the cuff off now,' to the PC. She seemed relieved to do so, grasping the opportunity to escape. The superintendent joined me in the van, another cop handing back my left hand so I could reattach it. I placed it on the bench next to me as yet another police officer joined us. He introduced himself as Chief Inspector Medley of Kent Police before falling silent to let the senior man talk.

'Am I free to go?' I asked.

The superintendent exhaled through his nose. 'Eyewitness reports say you were fighting a gang of men and that you were shooting blue light from your hands.'

'Am I free to go?' I repeated myself since he hadn't bothered to answer my question. He was trying to intimidate me, and I wasn't going to let it work. 'I ask again, because you didn't seem to hear me the first time.'

Now he pursed his lips and narrowed his eyes a little as if studying me. He answered my question though, 'No, Miss Aaronson, you are not free to go. There has been a lot of destruction of property this evening, two officers are on their way to hospital with concussion and you were involved in three other incidents in the last twenty-four hours. You wish to play the innocent card and act as if you could not be involved because you are a small woman with terrible injuries, but I read your army report a few minutes ago.'

'What army report?'

Again, he ignored my question. 'It portrays you as a loose cannon, Miss Aaronson, a person with documented authority issues. Who was the man you were with tonight?'

'I wasn't with anyone. I was attacked and a man came to defend me. We didn't exchange phone numbers.'

He lunged forward to jut his face up close to mine. 'Is this a joke to you?' he snarled, his voice several decibels louder. 'People are getting hurt. As I understand it, there are a dozen or more men buried under that mound of dirt over by the cathedral.' I wondered what they would find when they dug it up. 'You are clearly at the centre of something,' his voice softened again. 'Tell me what it is, Miss Aaronson. I only want to help you if I can. Any crimes you have personally committed will be considered differently if you help me to bring the people behind these terrorist attacks to justice.'

I had to suppress an unwelcome laugh that bubbled up at the suggestion I was the one committing crimes. 'Superintendent. If I knew what the hell was going on, I would tell you. I get why you don't believe that I am an innocent bystander, but I am not taking part in anything willingly. I was attacked this evening. Just like I was attacked outside the library this morning and just like I was attacked at the hospital last night.'

I could see that I was frustrating him and that he was doing his best to not let it show. He turned to his subordinate, inclining his head to say something but as he did a loud voice pierced the relative quiet outside.

Through a loudhailer, a man said, 'This area is now under the control of the Special Investigations Bureau. All police officers are hereby relieved of duty and the senior officer present must report to me immediately.'

The two men exchanged a glance. 'Who the hell are the Special Investigations Bureau?' asked the junior officer.

Squinting in his displeasure as he headed for the door, the Superintendent muttered, 'Some new bunch out of London. All I know about them is that no one knows anything about them, and they report directly to the Home Office.'

Both men clambered out and once again I asked, 'Am I free to go now?'

Neither even acknowledged my question as they walked away. However, as the cool air outside filtered in, I realised with a small snort of jubilation, that they left me without a guard. I crossed to the edge of the van to peer out.

An armoured van marked Special Investigations Bureau was pushing against the police barrier at North Gate. The police had used the natural funnel there to shut the crowd out which kept me and the police inside the barrier and next to the cathedral where all the action occurred earlier. The van had a top hatch with a large calibre machine gun mounted on top of it and the driver wasn't taking no for an answer. There were two more armoured vans behind it I noticed, just as a side door on the lead vehicle opened to dispense two men in suits. They paid no attention to the cops manning the barrier, sweeping by them as they wafted their ID wallets and never broke step. Half a dozen cops were moving to reinforce those at the barrier who were being so ineffective.

I could hear raised voices as the men from the Special Investigations Bureau insisted the entire area was now under their jurisdiction. My attention wasn't really on them though, it was on the fact that no one was minding me. I hadn't been read my rights and when I asked if I was free to go, he didn't answer, which I could take as a yes just as much as a no. Either way, I wasn't hanging around.

Slipping silently from the rear of the unguarded van, I crossed the pavement it was parked against to merge into the shadows. There were too many cops around for me to be able to walk away; I was inside a cordon, so my escape route was going to involve a wall somewhere. A few yards away, and nestled between North Gate and the cathedral, sat a small parade of shops. They had an enviable position for catching tourists, but that wasn't what got my attention. It was the black spot behind them, which turned out to be an alleyway that led around the back. They most likely used it to take out their trash so it came as no surprise when I found a wheelie bin to climb on. I went over a wall, thankful there was no additional barbed wire or anything there to stop me, and dropped down on the other side into the rear yard of a restaurant on the High Street.

No shouts followed me. There were no calls for me to stop. I edged along the side of the building to join the mass of confused and scared onlookers still crowding for a view. My head was down as I did my best to blend in with everyone else, my intention to walk calmly, but swiftly away from the area.

I didn't get very far before a voice calling my name stopped me.

Chapter 19

'Anastasia!' I heard the shout again.

I spun around this time and reached up to clamp my hand over Alex's mouth. 'Shhh!' I insisted.

Her cheeks coloured. 'Oh, yes, good point.'

'What are you still doing here?' I asked, grabbing her by the elbow to pull her along the road. Looking around, I noticed she was alone, 'Where's Abi?'

'Abi had to get home to her cats. I think the excitement was all a bit much for her, truth be told.' Alex could keep up with me easily, her long legs striding once for every two fast steps I took. I let her arm go but kept my pace up as I tried to look casual and uninteresting without slowing down. There were still people in the street to mingle in with and businesses a hundred yards away had diners in them oblivious to the excitement at the cathedral. 'I saw them cuff you and I just couldn't believe it. But I figured they would work out their mistake soon and let you go so I hung around. Then, when those other guys turned up, I spotted you sneaking away. Won't they come after you?'

'Probably, yes. Not tonight though and you saw what happened; the police cannot protect themselves against the magic shit getting thrown around, and they certainly can't protect me.'

'Holy smokes, Anastasia. You just ran away from the police. What are you going to do now?'

I couldn't deny the terror I felt at my current situation. Aside from having no idea what was going on, the police would be after me and two wizards were somehow fighting over me. I was having a strange couple of days, but I had names now: Sean McGuire and Otto Schneider. That had to get me somewhere. I slowed my pace and put my right hand up to stop Alex.

'Do you live alone?'

She looked startled by the question. 'Yes, why.'

'Because we need somewhere to go. My flatmate has already asked me to move out and the police will definitely think to look for me there.'

'Yes, good point.' She pulled a face as she thought the problem through. 'As long as you don't mind unicorns, you can crash at mine for as long as you like.'

'Unicorns?'

Alex had a thing for unicorns. I discovered this when I went through her front door. She lived within easy walking distance of the High Street and less than two hundred yards from the library, which made it convenient for work. Her apartment was in a new block of flat and handily near to the new railway station. Unicorns adorned every surface. In many shapes and sizes, in artwork that hung on the walls, in cushions on her couch and on a rug across the floor of her living room. It was as if the woman had bought every unicorn item she had ever seen. She saw me looking about and admitted her shame, 'It's become a bit much, hasn't it?'

My eyes wide, I said, 'Um.'

Her shoulders sagged. 'I know. I know.' She sounded defeated. 'I need to clear some of them out, but each one of them is so precious.'

'Do you have a boyfriend?' I asked tentatively.

'Sadly not. And I'm not sure what a new man would make of this place if I ever brought him back here.' Alex ditched her jacket and vanished, leaving me in the living room with the stable of unicorns. I thought she might have gone to the toilet but the obvious sound of a kettle being filled drew me to find her in the kitchen.

'Coffee?' she asked, as she plugged it in.

Two minutes later, I was online and staring at a photograph of Otto Schneider. Alex brought two steaming mugs of coffee to the table. It was getting late now, gone ten at least, and I was beginning to feel tired. The coffee was exactly what I needed to keep me going since sleep didn't feel like an option right now.

Looking over my shoulder, Alex read from the screen. 'He's a detective?'

'He used to be at least.' I was looking at a website for his business. It was still an operational website with a number and an email where I could contact him. I snatched up my phone and dialled his number.

I genuinely didn't expect him to answer, so his voice startled me when he said, 'Otto Schneider.'

'Mr Schneider, this is Anastasia Aaronson.'

'It's Herr Schneider,' he correctly me abruptly. 'Don't call this number again.' Then the line went dead, the ignorant git hanging up on me.

Huffing out an annoyed breath, I went back to the German webpages my search had turned up. A translate function changed them to English so I could read them – all it took was a few lines for me to work out that what I was seeing was much the same as Alex and Abi had showed me a few hours ago in the pub. These were the German equivalent of the same conspiracy websites though my search had picked up those which mentioned Otto Schneider.

There had been an incident in Bremen more than a year ago. Details were sketchy but one article accused him of being an eco-terrorist and staging a protest outside of the cathedral where he tore down a tree and wrought destruction to the area outside the ancient structure. Other forums hailed him as a man who was fighting alone against supernatural forces. On yet another forum an argument raged between two academics, one who was certain the end of days was coming – the biblical end of the world and what we were seeing was the start of that cataclysm, and another fellow who argued that this was nothing more than the next stage of evolution. His belief was that humans had always possessed the ability to perform what uneducated people referred to as magic, but was merely the manifestation of abilities we could not yet explain; a mobile phone to a Victorian would be deemed magic, he posited.

None of what I found gave me any indication why he was here and protecting me from the other man who remained an enigma. Sean McGuire didn't show up on social media, websites, or anywhere else. I got lots of hits for different Sean Mcguires, some of them famous, but I was fairly certain the man I wanted wasn't a Wall Street hedge fund manager or a Major League baseball player.

'No sign of him?' asked Alex as she returned to the table with two fresh mugs of coffee; our third of the night. It was closing in fast on midnight and she had been yawning for more than an hour.

'You should call it a night,' I told her. 'This doesn't take both of us.' When I looked up from my screen to see why she hadn't replied, it was obvious she was trying to work out how to say something. 'Spit it out,' I encouraged.

She pulled a sorry face. 'Do you think he will come here looking for you?'

A little ball of worry gripped my stomach. 'I hadn't thought of that. I should go.'

'Oh, no you don't!' she countered, moving her body to bar the door. 'We're in this together now. Girls united.'

It was nice to finally have a friend, but the likelihood of her getting hurt was too great. Pushing energy out of my centre, where I could feel the potential of it just waiting to be used, I filled my right palm with crackling pale blue light. 'I have a weapon, Alex. You do not, and I don't want anyone else to get hurt. You saw what they did outside the cathedral. Otto buried dozens of shilt with a spell. Imagine what they could do to us.'

Frowning in her annoyance, she glanced around her kitchen, snatched the toaster off the counter and yanked out the cable, then proceeded to swing it dangerously. I couldn't deny that I would want to avoid getting struck by the toaster, but Alex saw all the crumbs which were now flying out of it and stopped. 'Oh, bother,' she blushed. 'Maybe I have my old hockey stick somewhere in a cupboard.'

I couldn't help but smile, her attitude was what got our little island through the Second World War. 'I think I have to do this alone. It was dangerous of you and Abigail to follow me this evening. I have so many cuts and bruises already and I honestly don't know how I survived.'

'No,' Alex argued. 'You have to at least stay here the night. I'll sleep in front of the door if I have to. Try moving me with your tiny arms. I'm bloody heavy I'll have you know.' Now I did laugh, and I settled back into my chair, waving my hand in surrender.

I didn't know if Sean or Otto would come to Alex's place, but I didn't think they had a magical way to find me. Sean had tracked me to the hospital but that was after I fought the shilt there, so maybe he knew where to look for me. And he found me at the library, but again perhaps he knew I had a job there. This evening, I had found him, not the other way around and Otto seemed to be tracking Sean, not me.

'Hold on,' I said to myself as I remembered something.

'What is it?' Alex asked around another yawn.

'When they were fighting, Otto said something about having to kill Sean for killing someone else. I think it was multiple someone elses. There was something ...' I had to wrack my brain to remember what had been said. I wasn't exactly listening at this time. 'Sean said he would kill them all and something about Otto's mistake was in freeing them in the first place.' I thought some more while Alex waited patiently. 'Yes, that's it. Sean plans to kill them all; whoever they are, and said Otto gave them a punishment not a blessing.'

Alex wasn't able to follow my train of thought. 'What are you telling me?'

'Do you remember the Realm of False Gods forum Abi was showing us this afternoon. There were nutters on there who claimed to have lived in a different version of Earth. What if that is who Otto and Sean are fighting over. Otto freed a load of slaves from this other version of Earth. They get kidnapped from here and dragged through that shimmering pool of air thing. They cannot get back by themselves and they don't age, but then Otto goes and brings them back.'

'And Sean is hunting them down,' Alex finished my sentence with a hushed whisper. It made sense. Well, sort of anyway. It also felt like I was clutching at straws.

I shook my head; I just didn't know what to think, but I wasn't going to sit around and wait for Sean to have another attempt to grab me. He said he wanted to offer me employment. What kind of employment though?

Alex's phone pinged and she got up from her chair without even looking at it. 'Abi is here.' she announced leaving the room.

'Really?' I called after her. 'At this time?'

Chapter 20

'I found someone we need to talk to.' Abigail made her announcement as she set her handbag down on Alex's kitchen table. 'Ooh, is there any more of that coffee going around?'

'It's instant,' Alex admitted. I wanted to add that it was also terrible, but I held back from insulting my host.

Abigail had gone home from the High Street when she realised there was nothing more she could do. Unlike Alex, who lived within walking distance, she had to get a bus and then, once sobered up, had driven her car back to find us. Alex chose to text two hours ago to tell Abi I was at hers.

'What've you got?' I asked, as she got out her laptop.

'I found out who the man with the shield is. His name is Otto Schneider.' She sounded pleased with her detective work until I turned my screen slightly and showed her his website. Now crestfallen, she said, 'Oh. How did you work that out?'

'The other guy, the one in the big hood, his name is Sean McGuire. The two of them were helpful enough to use their names this evening.'

'That was helpful,' she agreed.

I had to frown at her as I asked, 'How did you work it out?'

Abigail waggled her eyebrows just as Alex set a steaming mug of black liquid next to her computer. 'Ah, well, I got clever and used the photograph we found earlier and put it onto all the live forums I could find. I said he had just saved my life and was clearly a supernatural, then asked if anyone knew who he was.'

'And you got a hit?' Alex asked, settling into a chair at the table opposite me.

Proudly, Abi said, 'I got three.'

She was being cryptic with the information as if building up to a big punchline. I didn't have the patience for that. 'What did they say, other than to give you his name?'

'Well, they all came back and said his name is Otto Schneider. But after that they wouldn't talk to me. I found him online straight away, but they wouldn't confirm how they knew him no matter what I wrote.'

'Where are they?' I asked.

Abi grimaced. 'None of them would tell me.' She looked at Alex and me, her face betraying that she thought their refusal to chat was odd. 'Honest, they were super secretive. It was as if they were hiding from someone or something.'

As the dread of her statement stole across me, I murmured, 'I need to know what they know. Any chance we can get an address?'

Abi and Alex exchanged a glance. 'We can probably reverse the IP to find where they live,' said Alex.

'Provided they are using their computer at home,' added Abi.

While they fiddled with that, I used my laptop to find the forum Abi had been using and reread the short chain of messages. Then I noticed the icon that showed the woman was currently online and crafted a message of my own:

Dear Inca151, Otto Schneider has come to my rescue twice now, though I have no idea why. I am able to create balls of blue energy in my right hand and hope that means something to you. A man called Sean McGuire is trying to take me with him. I need help.

120

I pressed send and watched the screen. My simple message revealed something I believed others wouldn't know about – the name of my assailant. I held my breath while I waited; one second, two seconds, then a little ellipsis symbol appeared to indicate Inca151 was typing.

What are you?

Three words. It wasn't the first time I had been asked that question. In fact, I think it was the third or possibly fourth time in twenty-four hours. I gave her my honest answer:

Just a woman. So far as I know. Yesterday, I stumbled across some shilt attacking someone and when I fought with them, I fired a pulse of energy out of my right hand. Then I found more of them attacking children in a hospital ward. This morning Sean attacked me, and it was Otto who saved me. I don't know him though; I don't know either of them, but I am certain Sean is coming back.

The ellipsis flashed on and off again, the three little dots appearing and disappearing as the person at the other end typed. It went on for ages, which made me think I was going to get a long answer. When the next message flashed into life, yet again it was just three words.

We should meet.

Before I could type a question asking where and when, an address flashed onto the screen. There was a single word after the address.

Hurry.

Chapter 21

U nable to take my eyes off the screen, I stuttered, 'Um, girls.'

Alex sighed. 'Abi and I don't really know what we are doing. Getting an address might take a while.'

I turned my laptop to show them. 'I already got it.'

Both women squinted at the screen. 'But that's just a few miles from here,' said Abigail.

I was pushing back my chair and getting up as I nodded. 'That's right. I need to go there, right now.'

'What if it's a trap?' asked Abi.

I hadn't considered that. 'It can hardly be worse than what I have endured so far. Sean will come for me again. I am certain of that. He wants to employ me, but that doesn't sound like a good career choice. I don't know who this Otto Schneider guy is, or whose side he is on. Or even if I can trust him, but I can't stay here. I tried to take the fight to them this evening and look at where that got me. If it is a trap, then I will at least save myself a whole load of running around.'

Alex snorted a laugh. 'That is one way of looking at it.' She also stood up, snagging her jacket from the counter where she left it earlier.

'I'm going alone this time,' I insisted.

Alex put her jacket on. 'The hell you are. Besides, how are you going to get there? You don't have a car unless there's one hidden in your backpack.'

'I'll get a cab.'

Abi shook her head vigorously. 'Girl's get raped in cabs by themselves. Happens all the time.'

Still arguing, I said, 'I think that's probably desperately drunk girls who don't have a magical hand cannon.' For added effect, I pushed a ball of crackling energy into my hand and held it aloft.

Alex pursed her lips. 'Nevertheless, I couldn't possibly let you go alone. We all go or I bar the door with my body and you have to try to move me.'

Exasperated but also relieved, I held up both hands in surrender. 'Okay, crazy ladies of the night it is. What kind of car do you have?'

Chapter 22

Alex revealed that her actual height is six feet two and a half inches, which in her words is, 'Really bloody tall for a woman.' Her mother was five feet five and her elder sister is only five feet six. I started to wonder if we were going to find out that she was part ogre or something which, honestly, wouldn't have shocked me given the continual weirdness since I arrived in Rochester.

Sadly, perhaps, her height came from her six-foot five-inch father. Either way, when she opened the door of an old-style Mini Cooper, I had to assume she drove it out of a sense of irony.

'How do you even get in?' I asked, watching her with wonder as she reversed awkwardly into the driver's seat bum first.

'It takes a bit of doing,' she admitted. 'Everyone says I should get something bigger.'

'You *should* get something bigger,' agreed Abigail.

'But it was an eighteenth birthday present from my dad, and he died before my next birthday, so this is that last thing I ever got from him.' Her seat was tilted back so she was resting at an angle that wasn't far off forty-five degrees, but she was in. I climbed in the back but had to sit behind the passenger because the driver's seat was all the way back and almost touching the back seat. Alex probably could have sat on the backseat and still driven the car. 'We would take Abi's car ...'

'Why don't we?' I asked.

'Because Abi has a two-seater,' said Abi, pointing out the window to a Triumph Spitfire in British Racing Green. She was all about style.

The engine of the tiny car roared to life, the stereo blasting out ACDC until Alex turned it quickly down. Then, just as she was about to put it in gear, I screamed for her to stop.

It was the mystery man from the hospital. I had all but forgotten him, convincing myself that I must have imagined it, but he had just moved between shadows, revealing his face and a haircut I would recognise anywhere.

Alex had a hand on her heart, 'Sweet lord, Ana!' The car stalled out, but there would be no time for escape by car when whoever he was could just throw magic at us. When he vanished in the children's ward, he left behind the same shimmering air I saw the shilt create so he had to be with them.

This was the next wave of attack!

'Get the door open!' I yelled at Abigail as I threw myself into the front of the car. There wasn't time to be nice and let her get out. I had to move now and be ready to defend the two women who were sitting ducks in the car. Abi squealed as she fought with her seatbelt release using one hand and the door release with the other.

Thankful for my child-like proportions for once, I slid over her lap and kicked the door open just as she pulled the handle. Power surged down my arm as I hit the ground with my left shoulder, rolled and came up. I had a ball of energy ready to throw and all the anger in the world to put behind it.

'Who are you?' I roared, advancing to get myself in front of the car. I got no answer back, squinting into the dark spot where I had just seen him. I wanted to throw the ball of energy anyway, only caution and concern that I might hit someone else or start a fire holding me back.

'Ana, what is it?' asked Abi. I could sense that she was hanging half out of the car. Alex probably holding on rather than going through the difficult process of climbing out again. I wasn't going to turn and look though, that would be the exact moment whoever was there would launch their attack.

Clenching my jaw, I growled, 'Screw it,' and let the ball in my right hand fly. In less than a second it hit the brickwork behind where I thought I had seen him and illuminated the area to show me that he had gone; escaped or retreated when I was clambering from the car. I waited a few more seconds, but no attack came, adding yet more confusion to how I already felt. Spinning back around to face the car, both women wore confused faces. 'You really didn't see him?' I got two blank looks. 'A man hiding in the shadows with a blonde hairdo that made him look like he used to hang out with Jesus?'

'Um, no,' said Abigail. 'There was no one there when I looked.'

'Dammit,' I swore. He had looked me right in the eyes and I knew it was the same man I saw last night at the hospital. I looked back at the darkness, wondering if he might have miraculously reappeared, then chastising myself for being surprised at his escape. In the last day, I had seen people fly using magic and create shimmering doors in the air that popped to nothingness after they went through them. Wanting to kick something, I stalked back to the car.

'We had better go before someone reports the light show,' Alex said neutrally. I think she was actually a little pissed off with me for scaring her, but I couldn't undo that now.

Chapter 23

Whoever Inca151 turned out to be, he or she lived in Allhallows. An odd little place on the beach was how Alex described it. It was ten or eleven miles, the girls agreed, and a straight line on one road almost the whole way there and back once we got across the river. They were conscious of my agitated state, but neither mentioned it as I constantly checked behind us and squinted into the darkness ahead. I found myself scanning hedgerows, expecting to see light reflect from the obsidian sword of a shilt just before he threw it through the window. It was just paranoia, an unwelcome reaction to the constant fighting and running of the last two days.

It was coming up on one in the morning when we got to the address. To my surprise, it wasn't a little cottage by the sea but a block of linked apartments; a big slab of concrete with concrete stairs leading up to them and concrete walkways running in front of all the doors. I associated such things with the inner city, not out here on the coast.

Exiting the car, I could instantly smell the salt in the air, a light onshore breeze carrying it. The temperature had dropped a few degrees which made it cool now, the warmth of summer long gone as we powered through autumn. I needed Abigail to get out so that I could extricate myself without having to climb over her again; an experience neither one of us enjoyed. However, as she undid her seatbelt, Alex reached for hers as well.

I grabbed her wrist. 'I need to do this bit alone. They come across as very skittish, so I don't want to spook whoever it is.'

Alex nodded. 'We'll wait in the car. Let us know if you are going to be long.' I genuinely expected to have to argue with her; it was a relief that I didn't but I worked out why just as I got to the door number I needed and heard both women trying to sneak along behind me.

I put my hands on my hips in a display of my frustration. 'The car was boring,' explained Alex. 'Are they there?'

'I don't know,' I replied, my tone dripping with irony. 'I haven't had the chance to knock yet.'

'But the door is open,' she pointed out.

I hadn't noticed, but she was right, the door was slightly ajar, and I didn't like that one bit. A ball of worry found its way to my belly. Did I knock and call out, or was it better to sneak in and see for myself?

Choosing the stealthy approach, I pushed the door open and peered into the gloom. I had to overcome an urge to call out, 'Hello,' into the dark as I stepped across the threshold. Alex and Abi made to follow to me, but this time I put my foot down, urgently hissing, 'Stay here and keep an eye out. If anyone comes, you let me know.'

Then I shut them both outside, closing the door to prove the lock still worked and hadn't been broken by someone forcing their way in. There were no lights on, but my stealthy steps didn't get me more than a few feet into the hallway before one flicked on ahead of me.

This time, I did speak, 'Hello?' I did my best to keep any nerves I felt from making my voice tremble.

I didn't get an answer. What I got was movement as someone stepped into the doorway ahead to show themselves. It was Otto Schneider. I froze for a moment, unsure how to react, but he wasn't being aggressive. If anything, he looked sad.

'He was right,' Otto said, his German accent clear though his English was perfect. 'I cannot be everywhere.'

He walked away from the door to disappear inside the room, making me follow to see where he had gone. Going further into the apartment brought an acrid smell to my nose. I didn't have to ask what was causing it because I reached the doorway and found Inca151 slumped on her couch with a softball sized hole burnt through the centre of her chest. She was a woman in her mid-twenties and tall though not nearly as tall as Alex. She was pretty and she had blond shoulder-length hair that ought to be lustrous, but it hung lifeless now as her chin slumped onto her chest.

'Sean did this?' I asked.

Otto nodded. 'Yes. I was too late to stop him.'

'Why? Who is he and why did he kill this woman?'

I didn't get an answer, I got a question instead, 'What does he want with you?'

'No.' I shook my head angrily. 'I have been getting attacked for the last two days. Ever since I arrived in this town and heard the shilt in my head, my life has been turned upside down. I want answers, not more questions.'

'Then I cannot help you. My only interest is in stopping Sean from killing more of those I helped. Given your obvious ancestry, I have no concern for your long-term safety.' He started toward the door to leave.

'Wait. What? What ancestry. What do you know about me?' I chased after him, but he swivelled his torso as he walked, moving his hands as I had seen both him and Sean do before. I saw what he was doing but couldn't react fast enough to do anything before my feet were swept out from under me by a gust of knee-height wind.

He didn't even break stride when he raised his voice, 'I don't know which side you are on, little girl. You may yet be my enemy.'

I was scrambling back to my feet to go after him when he opened the door and went out. Light from a lamp outside silhouetted him for a moment as both Alex and Abi swore in surprise at his sudden appearance. I wanted to shout for them to stop him, but they weren't my troops and doing so would just place them in danger; I had already established I was no match for the two wizards.

Otto leapt over the walkway railing to drop two stories to the ground below but when I got there to join the two women looking over the side at him, he was nowhere to be seen. We hadn't even heard him hit the ground.

'What happened?' asked Alex. 'Are you alright?'

I grabbed Abi's coat and pushed Alex toward the stairs. 'We need to get out of here.'

They came with me but argued as they walked. 'What about the person you were going to meet? Were they there?' asked Abi.

Alex gasped. 'Or was it him all along? Why would he bring you here and then vanish again?'

I did my best to explain as I continued to push them along, 'Inca151 is a woman and she is dead. Otto claims Sean killed him but I'm not so sure that's true. What is it they say on detective shows? The last person to see the body is probably the killer. Well, I found him in the room with her and she didn't look like she had been dead very long.'

Alex asked, 'You think Otto killed her?'

Chapter 24

A t the UK headquarters of the Supernatural Investigation Alliance in London, Commissioner Marcus Swinton had questions and didn't like the answers he was getting. He was a long serving military commander, seconded into the SIA at forty-two and glad of it because he was getting bored with the lack of action; there were no wars anymore. He had joined up right before Iraq and Afghanistan, then had come Syria and other minor deployments after that. It was all done now though, the few soldiers on peacekeeping in Zannaria would get a medal but the glory days of his youth were not available to the troops joining now. The SIA was much more like it; a clandestine organisation who were known by a cover name by those few who even knew about them. He had direct access to the Home Secretary, the only person he took orders from, with the exception of the SIA high command in the States.

They knew a supernatural event was coming; agents such as Otto Schneider assured them of it and helped them prepare. They weren't ready though, that wasn't in dispute, but they couldn't control the timeline and the recent shilt attacks in Rochester were the first in that territory.

'You think the woman is of no consequence?' he asked.

'That is not what I said,' Otto corrected him. 'I said that she may be of no consequence. The bigger issue, and the one on which we must focus, is Sean McGuire. He will continue to kill the familiars I freed until he is stopped.'

'How many has he killed now?' asked Swinton's deputy Michelle Parker, a Caribbean woman whose grandparents came to England in the early fifties. Her black hair was beginning to turn grey, and she was ten years Swinton's senior though he held the higher rank. It wasn't something that bothered her.

Otto turned his attention her way. 'In this country or worldwide? It's six in this country.' He answered his own question. 'You have to get to them quicker. They are weak by themselves but together they will make a force to stand against the demons.'

Swinton felt aggrieved at being called out on their lack of success. 'You shouldn't have sent them home the way you did, releasing them to go about their lives.'

'You shouldn't have suppressed their voices.' Otto snapped in response, instantly angry that they would turn this on him. 'I set them free so the world would have evidence of the demons and their intention to return. You could have educated the population to guard against the shilt.'

'The population isn't ready,' said a new voice. Swinton had to stop himself from springing to attention, years of muscle memory making his leg twitch at the Home Secretary's voice.

'Home Secretary,' he said, his greeting echoed by Michelle who crossed the room to shake the statesman's hand.

'What happened in Rochester?' he asked, clearly expecting a full report.

Otto spoke before the commissioner got the chance. 'An old enemy sprung an attack and I was unable to defeat him.'

'Unable?' repeated the Home Secretary with exaggerated surprise. 'I thought you were invincible.'

'I have no time for foolish word games,' sighed Otto sliding off the table he had chosen to rest on. 'I am immortal, not invincible. Had I employed the tactics I needed to eliminate him tonight, there would have been loss of life.'

'I understand that there was loss of life,' the Home Secretary snapped.

Swinton stepped in, not wanting to see either party upset. 'Those killed were all identified as shilt.'

'Yes, I buried a load of them. Your men were able to recover them without the population seeing, I suppose.' Otto made his disagreement with the policy of secrecy no secret.

Swinton reported to his boss. 'Sir, there were no human casualties, though several people were hurt including two police officers.'

The Home Secretary nodded. 'Good.' His attention shifted to the wizard. 'Every government involved in the Alliance is unified in their belief that the world will pull itself apart if it gets the slightest whiff of what we believe is to come. Looting, rioting, panic buying on unprecedented levels will occur. Many will die and nothing will have been achieved.'

'Yes. Your plan is to keep them in the dark until the demons return and either kill or enslave them. What will that achieve, Home Secretary?'

Ever the politician, the Home Secretary had an answer ready. 'Your plan is to tell them the demons are coming so they can say goodbye to their loved ones. What will that achieve, Herr Schneider? It is not as if knowing that it is a demon stealing their child will stop it from happening. They will be just as powerless as before.'

'No,' Otto argued. 'It will give credence to the idea that supernaturals are among us; then we can encourage them to come forward. We have no idea when the death curse will fail but we do know that the demons will be on us in moments, Beelzebub bringing the full might of his assembled army against us.'

'An army you claim to exist and wish for us to prepare against with no evidence. By your own admission you have not seen it and do not know how many demons there are.'

How Otto rued letting that slip. He wasn't going to defend himself though. 'Home Secretary, when the demons bite your arse, you will be at the back of a long line of people who refused to listen.'

'Why do you work with us then?' asked the politician, smiling as if he had just made an argument winning point.

With a sad smile, Otto said, 'Because my hope springs eternal that one day you may all see sense and save yourselves.'

Both sides lapsed into silence as they considered what to say next. Swinton, keen to look like he was in charge of his own department, cleared his throat. 'I need you to convince me why we shouldn't bring in the woman, Anastasia Aaronson.'

'Because the other side want her,' Otto replied, as if it were obvious. Swinton didn't follow, neither did his deputy or the Home Secretary. Seeing their creased brows, he explained. 'Demons only take people for one reason: to use as a familiar. But if that was their intention, they would have just taken her. The demons don't like to come here, it makes them weak, but they will for a short period of time if it suits their purpose. Therefore, we can assume they want her for something else. Aaronson possesses some power though it is entirely untrained, but I don't think she knows what she is.'

'What is she?' interrupted Swinton.

'Beats me. She can summon source energy and no human alive has ever been able to do that according to the demons. She is not an angel though; her injuries show her mortality, so she will die with one blast of hellfire just like anyone else. Whatever she is, she isn't a witch, she doesn't appear to have any elemental magic ability and I haven't seen her shift or conjure or anything else.'

'She's something new then?' asked Michelle.

Otto nodded, thinking to himself as he repeated what she said, 'She is something new.'

'I think we should bring her in for her own safety,' advised the Home Secretary.

Otto sneered at him this time. 'You mean for your safety because you want to lock her down until you can work out if she is dangerous.' The Home Secretary was about to argue but Otto cut over the top of him. 'I want to know why the demons want her, which you will not find out if you bring her in here. They are not as dumb as you want to believe. They have humans working for them in this mortal realm, you should believe that. Maybe even within the Alliance itself.'

'They are capable of espionage and subterfuge?' The Home Secretary was astounded by the concept.

Otto wanted to bury his face in his hands. 'They are not dumb animals. They ran the planet for thousands of years. Not only that, they ran it better than we have. If they weren't prepared to enslave humanity as they carve up our borders to create a singular nation ruled by a singular being, then I would probably side with them.'

The Home Secretary's eyes came out on stalks and his lips flapped as he tried to form a sentence.

'Don't bother,' Otto told him as he headed for the door. 'If you go after the woman, I will stop giving you my help and make my own army to fight the false gods.'

'Stop him!' The Home Secretary was incensed by the German's impudence. 'How dare he threaten us?'

Swinton moved to block his boss's path as he stalked after the wizard. The Home Secretary clearly wasn't used to being on the back foot and was going to say or do something rash if not stopped. 'We need him, sir. Not the other way around.'

'What?' The Home Secretary's eyes were flicking between Otto's back and the head of his SIA department.

'He's an immortal wizard, sir. He doesn't need anyone. He agreed to work with the SIA in Germany and by extension, all other departments, but it's on his terms, sir. Not ours. When the fight comes, we will need him.' Otto had left the room, the situation effectively diffused so far as Commissioner Swinton was concerned.

However, the Home Secretary was far from satisfied. 'We need him, eh? We shall soon see about that.'

Otto didn't hear the Home Secretary's final comment, nor would he have cared if he had. Petty men with insignificant concerns never penetrated the surface. He had fried bigger fish and knew he wasn't nearly half done yet. Leaving the building, he considered his next move. Sean was almost impossible to track or predict; catching him at the library had occurred only because he heard of the shilt attack at the hospital from the Alliance, Swinton proving he could be useful. From there all he had to do was watch the ley lines and react when someone pulled a significant amount of power through one.

Sean was wily and fast though, escaping Otto even though it was daylight and he couldn't open a portal. It happened again at the cathedral. He expected to be able to close with Sean. Magic for magic they were well matched. Sean was far older, with more than a century of experience, but Otto knew he couldn't be killed and that made a lot of difference in a fight – he would take risks that others wouldn't because he knew for him, they weren't risks. His sole intention was to kill the other wizard. Offering Sean a way out, a way to return to humanity hadn't gone well and Sean was now targeting the familiars Otto freed from the immortal realm. Otto needed to kill him, and he had a plan for how he would do it if he could get close enough. The trouble was being close enough to see when Sean pulled on a ley line to power his magic. He had lied about the woman, Anastasia Aaronson. She might be safer in Alliance hands. It might be safer for the Alliance too, but he needed her out there so that Sean would come for her. She was Otto's bait.

What Otto hadn't told the commissioner or his boss, the Home Secretary, was that a demon, most especially Daniel, wouldn't send a familiar to get a familiar when he was so adept at doing it himself. Which either meant that Daniel didn't know what Sean was doing, or more likely, Daniel was doing something his fellow demons wouldn't like, in which case the woman must be of particular value.

What that value was he couldn't guess, since her power appeared to be quite limited and she had terrible injuries, but whatever it was, Sean would come back for it and that meant Otto needed to be nearby.

Chapter 25

I crashed for the night at Alex's. I didn't really want to, but I had to acknowledge there was nowhere else to go unless I booked into a hotel and I knew I would have a fight with Alex if I even suggested it. Abigail went home with a promise to see us both at the library tomorrow. I smiled and bade her goodnight, but I knew I wasn't going to work in the morning. At a brand-new job, as I tried to carve out a new career, I was already skipping days. They wouldn't fire me, not yet at least. I think they knew what they were getting when they took on a woman missing two limbs, but my failure to appear wouldn't be received well I was sure, and I made sure to email Professor Grayhawk before I went to sleep.

However, sleep didn't come. Lying on Alex's couch, which I had to fight her for, the crazy woman trying to be the best host and giving up her bed when she clearly wouldn't fit on the couch and I had room to spare, I just couldn't get my mind to switch off. The woman I saw this evening had been murdered but I had no way of knowing if Otto had done it or Sean. I wanted to believe it was Sean; Otto had intervened to my benefit twice now and asked nothing in return, whereas Sean attacked me the first time; an apology didn't make up for that, and he sided with the shilt who I knew to be happily murderous and content to prey on children. Sean was a bad guy; the jury was out on Otto.

Regardless, I still didn't know what Sean wanted of me, but I felt certain he hadn't given up on his plan to employ me. I felt like the goat in *Jurassic Park*, just waiting for the T-Rex to eat me.

When I awoke to find sunlight streaming through the window, I realised fatigue had finally won the battle against alertness. It was a good thing; a soldier should always sleep when the chance presents itself. I had chosen to sleep with both my prosthetics on, convinced a shilt horde would burst through Alex's door while I slept. Now the sun was up, I felt I could risk taking them off. I needed to massage the stumps, it was part of the desensitising process but also, they just hurt after a while.

By the time Alex found me, I was dressed again, yesterday's clothes having to suffice since I wasn't getting to my own wardrobe anytime soon. I would buy new things today when I got the chance. But what should I do with my day? If I went to work, would I be endangering other people? I craved the normality and boredom a job presented. Even if I wasn't luring trouble to the library, would the police be waiting for me there?

In some ways, I should be thankful that I didn't have to work out what to do with my day, the decision was made for me when someone started thumping on Alex's door. She was still wearing pyjamas, men's ones I assumed from the fit and the size, but she had an awkward look on her face which made it clear she didn't want to answer the door. I was already dressed, so I went.

The thumping had been swiftly followed by, 'Police, open up,' delivered loud enough for all the neighbours to hear. The shout made me pause but only for a half second. There was no point putting it off and nothing to be gained by trying to escape them. Pulling my hood up to shroud my face, I opened the door with the safety chain on.

DS Spencer was outside, and he had a female officer with him. Both were in plain clothes, though the black female officer made her clothes look good in contrast to DS Spencer who appeared to have slept in his.

He gave me a pleasant smile. 'Good morning, Miss Aaronson. Would it be possible to have a moment of your time?'

This was not what I expected. His attitude caught me by surprise and I had to ask if I was being led over a metaphorical trapdoor. It wasn't my house so he could keep hoping if he wanted to be invited in. Through the crack in the door I said, 'You have my attention.'

'Can we come in?' he asked, his voice dripping with honey.

Enjoying myself, I told him, 'No. This isn't my place, so I have no right to invite you inside, and my host is getting showered and changed ready for work. What is it you would like to ask me?'

His smile didn't falter, but his partner's did. 'DS Spencer, what are we doing here?' she asked, impatient to be somewhere else.

Ignoring her, he kept his eyes on me. 'Miss Aaronson I am worried about you. I understand that you were involved in a third incident last night, one where some police officers were hurt, and property was destroyed. I hoped you might be willing to talk to me now. If there are people after you, I can help.'

His partner stiffened. 'DS Spencer a word if you please.'

Without turning away, DS Spencer smiled again and held up his index finger, 'I'll be just a moment.' Then a flicker of annoyance crossed his face right before he turned around to join his colleague a few feet away.

I didn't want to be curious, but I was, so I closed the door enough to get the chain off and opened it so I could better listen to their hushed conversation. They were arguing about something, the woman gesticulating that they should leave right now and looking quite angry. He was playing the innocent card, questioning why she was getting so excited.

I strained to hear and picked up something she said, 'It was a simple enough order to follow, Ralph. We either go now or I will have to report it. Otherwise I am complicit.'

'Report it then,' he snapped. 'I don't let criminals go just because some unnamed order comes down from on high.'

Her eyes flared but she didn't bother to argue any further; she turned about, offered him some advice involving several unladylike words and walked away. She was going to wait for him in the car.

Alone now, DS Spencer turned back around to face me, his smile returning. I wasn't buying any of it though. 'Still think I'm the criminal then?

The smile dropped away. 'I know you're involved, Miss Aaronson. Call it policeman's intuition. What I want to know is why I have been ordered to ignore your case? You went out of a window to avoid me yesterday, caused a whole load more trouble in town by the cathedral last night, yet after four incidents in a single twenty-four-hour period, the police are not allowed to investigate. Do you know what that means?'

I really didn't so I said, 'Could you enlighten me please?'

Mockingly, he replied, 'It means you are in far more trouble than you realise. Another organisation has claimed an interest in you; that is the only reason the police would ever back off.' He changed his tone again, this time imploring. 'Anastasia, if you voluntarily surrender yourself to my custody and tell me who is behind this, I promise to do my best to get you protection.' I noticed that he used my first name for the first time, and I could see that whatever was motivating him to disobey his order to stay away from me, it wasn't anything to do with protecting me.

'Ralph,' I replied, using his first name as well, 'you cannot protect me from the two men who caused the destruction outside the cathedral last night; they are both wizards.' He got a beaming smile as I delivered my line and I almost raised my right hand to show him my own 'magic' though I thought better of it at the last moment.

Irritation made his face twitch and that made my smile even broader. 'You can have it your way, Miss Aaronson.' Without a further word, he turned and walked away, reaching the stairs and vanishing from sight. I went back inside and shut the door.

'Who was that?' asked Alex, now dressed for work and passing me on her way to the kitchen.

I smiled again. What I had just learned shouldn't please me, but it was the first bit of decent news I'd been given since I arrived. 'It was an unfriendly detective. The police have some kind of ban that stops them investigating me. It means I can go back to my place this morning.'

Alex had a loaf of bread in her hands but wasn't doing anything with it as my news sunk in. 'The police cannot investigate you?' As she repeated my words, she was considering what they might mean. 'You think that has something to do with the guys in suits last night? Social media is going crazy because half of the High Street is blocked off. People can't get to work. It takes some clout to do that.'

'They'll be recovering the bodies of the shilt Otto buried last night, and yes, I think it has everything to do with the guys from last night.' On my phone I searched Special Investigation Bureau, the results filling my screen instantly. My eyes danced as I read the first article. It was on an official police website which stated the SIB were a branch of counter-terrorism police. That made sense, but when I looked at some of the other search results, I found they connected with Abi's conspiracy theory sites which claimed the SIB was a public front for a different organisation involved in covering up supernatural activities.

When I told Alex what I found, she said, 'That makes sense, I guess. If there are super-natural creatures killing people and kidnapping people and threatening humanity, then I would expect the government to cover it up. How could they not?'

'But how long can they keep it a secret?' I asked

'Is it a good or bad thing?' asked Alex. 'If people find out what you are, could you even go to work?'

A hopeless laugh escaped my lips. 'What I am. Everyone keeps asking me what I am, and no one seems to know. You're right though. My injuries,' I wafted a hand at my scarred face, 'and this are enough to make people shy away from me. I don't need to give people more reason to cross the street.'

Alex checked her watch. 'I had better get going. What are you going to do today?'

'I'm heading back to my flat. The police found me here so anyone else looking for me will be able to also; it's no longer a hiding place, but if the police are no longer looking for me ... I might come by work later as well, just to check in with poor Professor Grayhawk. He hired an assistant and I haven't done a minutes' work yet.'

Alex grabbed her handbag, checked she had her keys and started toward the door. 'Look, stay as long as you want. There's food in the fridge and water in the tap for tea and coffee. I'll be back around five if you are still here.'

I thanked her and watched her go but I was planning to leave myself in just a few minutes. A plan had been forming in my head since the moment DS Spencer revealed he wasn't allowed to bother me now. It seemed probable that someone else was now watching me, but so long as they didn't try to stop me, I couldn't care less.

A few minutes later the charge on my phone hit one hundred percent and I went out the door, locking it with the key Alex gave me and sticking it back under the door for her to find later. I had to go shopping, I had to make a phone call and I had to do something very, very illegal.

Today was going to be fun.

Chapter 26

The phone call was to Otto Schneider, to the number still listed on his website. When I called it yesterday and he hung up on me, I hadn't expected it to still be live; that it was shocked me. I saved the number under *crazy wizard dude* and pulled it out of my contact list now. I flicked my head to sweep my hair to one side as I put the phone to my ear and realised it was the first time I had done that since Zannaria. I cut my hair short to go there; desert environments are terrible for long hair, fine dust combines with sweat to create a mud-like product so like most of the men, I had my hair shorter than it had been at any point since birth. Now it was growing back to my normal length and that, at least, was something to be happy about.

'Otto Schneider.' His simple answer filled my ear.

'Otto, this is Anastasia, the girl with the missing hand,' I added quickly in case he didn't connect the dots. 'I want to work with you.'

There was no sound from the other end at all, not even breathing, then carefully, he said, 'Go on.' Him hanging up on me like he did yesterday had been a distinct possibility but with that hurdle negotiated I could hit him with the short speech I worked out in my head.

'I am not your enemy, Otto. At least I have no reason to believe that I am, but I know that you are fighting Sean, so siding with you is in my best interest. He has attacked me twice already.'

'What is special about you?' Otto's direct question caught me by surprise. I had been about to sell him on the idea that the enemy of my enemy might not be my friend but perhaps we could be temporary allies. I wanted to ask him questions if nothing else since he clearly had some idea what was going on.

Instead of that, I said, 'I can shoot blue orbs of energy from my hand.' It was the most honest answer I could give.

'Yes, you can,' he replied slowly. 'But you don't know how, do you?' He was curious at least. Even though I had no reason to trust him, and knew that he might be a serial killer, I would answer all his questions if he gave me a chance to.

'Can we meet? I am going home to prepare for Sean in case he comes for me again.'

'He will,' Otto assured me. 'As soon as the sun sets or some time thereafter. To attempt to grab you in public indicates a sense of urgency on his part. Now that he knows I am here he will come with as much support as he can get and that means a return tonight.'

'You mean more shilt?'

'Almost certainly, but he may enlist the help of other familiars or other creatures. He has no concern for human life so may employ tactics that will divide our attention. If we are to defeat him we must care not for casualties around us.'

Now he sounded like the sociopath serial killer many forums claimed he was. I was sticking my head in the lion's mouth, but I didn't feel like I had a lot of choice. I gave him the address for Sarah's apartment, and he disconnected after telling me he would arrive later.

What the hell did later mean?

Chapter 27

I needed some very specific items that one can find in everyday shops, but only if you have the right kind of shops to look in. Bought individually the products were harmless, once combined they made handy little grenades and I was going to use them to blow Sean's junk off. Having been a law-abiding citizen my whole life, I was about to make explosives, and I was planning murder.

The concept of killing Sean didn't bother me; I had contemplated such things many times as a soldier, but back then it had been my function and the targets were essentially faceless. Now I had to consider how the authorities were going to view it. 'If they catch me,' I said to myself for the umpteenth time since I made the decision to go all out.

The journey from Alex's place to Sarah's apartment took me through Rochester High Street where I found the first item on my list in a florist shop. The two middle-aged ladies looked surprised at my request for saltpetre, but they had a supply and took sympathy on the poor girl with the scarred face which I made a point of showing them. I said I needed it to make a poultice for my scars, basically daring them to not give me what I wanted by playing on a person's natural reluctance to discuss terrible wounds.

I bought lighter fluid in three different newsagents, rather than attempt to buy that amount in one place and look suspicious – who needs that much lighter fluid unless they are an arsonist? Charcoal in briquette form wasn't available anywhere on the High Street, nor were the base ingredients to make sulphur though I was able to find nitric acid in a chemist.

Light bulbs came from a small convenience store along with a bumper pack of toilet rolls, but with Rochester's parade of shops exhausted, I needed to ask directions to find a hardware store. It was walking distance, the Indian man in the newsagents assured me, and he was right, I guess, but it still took me an hour to get there.

A rumbling stomach pulled me into a small café when I caught the smell of bacon on my way past, so by the time I finally had all the items I needed and got back to Sarah's place, a large chunk of the day was gone and I had a lot of work to do.

The practice of making grenades was just one of the many things I learned in the build-up training before deployment to Zannaria. Even though we were going on a peacekeeping mission, they knew we might meet hostility and felt we ought to have all the skills we might require. Too often in the past had the government sent in its troops without the firepower to ensure they would not be opposed.

That was how I came to be in Sarah's kitchen cooking up explosives. Black powder is a simple and relatively inert compound to mix. Getting the balance of ingredients right is the tricky bit and I couldn't find a set of kitchen scales so had to eyeball it.

One of the key ingredients is sulphur, which you cannot just buy over a counter. But you can buy sodium thiosulphate which can be dissolved in water and then mixed with nitric acid. It takes a couple of hours, but the sulphur will settle to the bottom of the beaker.

While I waited for the sulphur to settle in the nitric acid, I got a shower and changed, picking out clothes I would be comfortable to get arrested in: stretchy blue jeans, tan Timberland boots, a capped-sleeve t-shirt and another hoody, this time a black one with a Hogwarts symbol on the back. It was odd that my messed-up memory couldn't tell whether I had ever seen the Harry Potter movies or read the books, but I knew who he was.

Feeling fresh, clean, and as ready as I was going to get, I checked the sulphur solution, accepted that it was going to take another hour or more and devoted that hour to making three petrol bombs using the lighter fluid and light bulbs. I had a dozen light bulbs, but they felt more fragile than I expected so I stopped at three. To ignite them I would use my magic as an ignition source. Each light bulb, half filled with lighter fluid, would need to be fixed above the ground somehow. I realised that I had forgotten to buy duct tape which caused a frenzied search of the house, the item I needed finally revealing itself in a drawer in Sarah's bedroom. It was with reluctance that I went through her things and hoped she wouldn't realise that was what I had done.

When I was content that the sulphur was ready, I moved onto the next stage which was to make the charcoal powder. I had to crush it to a powder by hand using a Pyrex bowl and a fork because Sarah didn't own a kitchen mixer either. The sulphur and charcoal combined gave me the fuel and I used saltpetre as an oxidizer. The powder I then packed into cardboard tubes I took from the middle of the pack of toilets rolls, doubling them up to make a thick outer wall and using duct tape to seal both ends. They were quick and dirty and had no ignition device. I planned to get around that problem by shooting blue orbs of energy at them just like the lighter fluid bombs. In a battle zone I would have added shrapnel; nuts and bolts or bits of gravel, anything that would do damage. It was an ugly thing to create, but none of that went into these. I thought the possibility of civilian casualties was too great plus a close-up explosion ought to have the desired effect which was to wound and temporarily disable.

When Otto Schneider walked into the kitchen without knocking on the front door or even making a sound as he approached, my nervousness over what I was doing made me almost drop the dozen grenades just as I was packing them into my backpack.

'Holy shit! You scared the living crap out of me. How did you get in?'

He looked at me like I was acting odd. 'I'm a wizard,' he replied as if his answer told me everything. 'What are you doing?'

'Making bombs.' I turned so I could look directly at him. 'I have a lot of questions I would like answers to, Herr Schneider. Would you be good enough to answer them?'

He stared directly into my eyes, holding my gaze without speaking for several seconds. It felt like he was measuring me. Finally, he said, 'No. I don't entirely trust you.'

A frown creased my forehead. 'You don't trust me? As far as I know, you are a serial killer.'

'Then given my abilities, it seems foolhardy to tell me where you live. I will tell you that I intend to kill Sean McGuire and that I am here because I believe he will come for you again.'

'What does he want me for?'

'That I cannot tell you.' When Otto saw my face filling with anger, he added. 'Because I do not know.'

I squinted at him. 'Then tell me why you feel the need to kill him.'

This time he pursed his lips as he cast his eyes down and to the right, making a decision that yet again turned out to be a no. 'It's a personal matter I have no wish to discuss. I will tell you that he has killed a lot of innocent people and will kill many more if he isn't stopped.'

'So he's the serial killer?'

'Yes, although I believe he sees himself as a soldier or, at worst, an executioner.' Otto's attention was divided between talking to me and looking in kitchen cupboards as he rooted around for something.

'What are you looking for?' I asked.

He pulled out a deep drawer containing saucepans, selecting a small milk pan which he set on to the gas hob. 'Just this.' As I watched, he stripped off ten rings, all the same and all silver though the sizes differed. He dropped one of them into the pan and then added water. Anticipating me, he said, 'You're about to ask what I am doing. The shield you saw me use to deflect the lightning Sean conjured is a defensive spell I developed some time ago. I connect the rings to my body using a drop of my blood.' He jabbed his finger with the tip of a small knife. I watched in fascination as he dripped his blood into the pan and set a flame beneath it. 'The shield is only good for one or two uses before it burns out, so I have a bunch of them.'

When the water began to boil, I watched as the wizard closed his eyes and reopened them. Staring down at the bubbling water, he moved his hands and then his lips, whispering a word just as a spark of magic lit the inside of the pan. Then he poured it out and repeated the process for the next ring.

A thought occurred to me. 'At the library, how did you know where to find me?'

He didn't take his eyes from the pan as he finally answered one of my questions. 'I didn't find you. I found Sean. I can see when people use magic and I happened to be in the area because I was curious about the shilt attacks last night. There was a surge in a ley line, I went to investigate and found Sean about to kill you. I didn't realise you were supernatural until you asked about my shield. No one else can see it, you know?'

'I didn't know. Though I got that impression. My friends see people when they look at the shilt. Why is that?'

Now Otto's attention did waiver. 'You can see through their enchantments, can't you?'

I shrugged. 'When I look at them, I see ugly lizard people. What do you see?'

'I have the ability to engage a second sight, sort of like a filter that focuses on magic. Otherwise I see them as normal people but with an aura around them.'

'An aura?'

'Yes. You have one too. Yours isn't like mine though. Or anyone else's I have ever seen.'

'In what way?' I didn't know I, or anyone else, had a visible aura, but now that I did, I was worrying about why mine was different.

'Tell me about your family, your grandparents. What did they do for a living? Do you re-member anything about them that would make you believe they were also supernatural?'

I pointed to my head. 'I have no memory of my family. I don't know anything about them.'

'Really?' he replied sceptically.

A little annoyed that he doubted me, my response came out snippier than I intended. 'Yes, thank you.' I lifted my hood back and pulled my hair to one side to show him my scar. 'I have a piece of metal in my brain from a land mine. It's really inconvenient.'

Otto stared at me for a heartbeat, then finished what he was doing, the need for conversation now gone so far as he was concerned.

I needed to ask one more question; one which was burning me up. 'What am I? My voice came out quiet and meek, so it sounded like I was pleading for information, which I was, really.

He stopped moving but didn't face me as he slipped the ten rings back onto his fingers and thumbs. I thought he wasn't going to reply, but he did, 'I don't know. You have magic within you, but you are not like anything I have come across before. When did your powers manifest?'

'Two days ago.'

'Really? How old are you?'

'Twenty-three.'

Otto considered what I had told him for a moment. 'You never had any magical or unexplainable experiences when you were younger?'

I pointed to the scar again. 'No memory.' It was sadly true that if I had been doing magic as a child, I simply couldn't remember. Maybe I had always made blue orbs in my right hand. I had no way of knowing now.

Accepting that he wasn't going to get any answers from me, he leaned back against the counter. 'We need to prepare for Sean. He will come at sundown, so we have less than an hour now.'

I glanced at the clock, startled by how much of the day had slipped by while I made explosives. I desperately wanted to ask him more questions now that he had finally started talking, but just as my brain told me Sarah would be coming through the door any moment, I heard it open.

She called out, 'Hello?' I could hear her taking off her heels and her coat by the door.

I hadn't considered how I was going to play this and hadn't replied to her last message where she asked me to move out. 'Hi, Sarah,' I replied, leaving the little kitchen so she could see me. I felt a bit embarrassed, as if I were trespassing and I was here with a man she didn't know. 'Um, Sarah ...' I began but she cut me off.

'God, Ana, I'm so sorry about that message I sent you. It was really shitty of me to ask you to move out after you got attacked. Are you okay?' Her cheeks were bright red, displaying the shame she claimed to feel.

Changing what I had planned to say, I went with, 'I'm a bit battered and bruised. I'm glad I don't have to get into a fight about staying here though, that would have been ... difficult.'

She cringed. 'Yeah, sorry. I overreacted. Would you like a glass of wine?' she asked, adding, 'I need one,' as she moved around me in the narrow hallway on her way to the kitchen. She was going to squeal when she found Otto in there!

I rushed to catch up. 'Sarah, this is ...' No one. The pan was still on the stove, but the wizard was nowhere in sight.

'This is?' she asked, opening the refrigerator to pluck a half empty bottle from the door.

Thinking fast, I said, 'Um, this is a great time for a glass of wine and proper chat but I was just leaving actually. I, ah, I have a date.'

'A date?' her expression was doubtful for a second before she realised she was questioning my ability to pick up a partner. 'Oh! Well, good for you. Where did you meet ... him?' she asked, the question's meaning clearly two-fold.

'Yes, it's a guy,' I told her, not that I thought she cared either way. 'It was at the library. It's not really a date though,' I told her, scrambling now to concoct a story I would remember later. 'It's just a male co-worker who offered to meet after work to go through some work stuff. I'm hoping to impress them with what I can do. He is cute though,' I embellished to make my lies sound more realistic I hoped.

'Are you going now?'

Seeing my chance for a fast exit, I picked up my backpack. 'Yes, I had better get going.'

Sarah saw the heft of the homemade grenades. 'Wow, that thing looks heavy. What have you got in there?'

'Books,' I replied quickly. 'Just books. It's a library thing.'

Sarah was no longer interested in my life, she had a cupboard open to get a glass for her wine and her back to me, so I called out that I was going, got a, 'Good luck,' in response and went out the door.

My legs felt leaden as I went down the stairs. There was a big fight ahead of me whether I wanted to take part or not. The police couldn't help me, not without getting hurt for no good reason. I couldn't hide, or, at least, I couldn't see anything to be gained by hiding, and I felt all alone and very lost. Otto was nowhere to be seen, not that I felt sure he was even on my side, but I hoped he would reappear soon.

In the meantime, I chose a battle ground. Too much time had elapsed, the sun was already dipping so I couldn't get away from the urban sprawl around me. The best I could do was find an open patch of ground near the river. It was less than a hundred yards from Sarah's apartment, but also fifty yards from the nearest house. If he was coming at sundown, I would need to be ready.

I was going to create a kill box.

Chapter 28

C hoosing the ground on which I would fight gave me some advantage because I could prepare it and be familiar with it. Such tactics are in the battle commander's handbook and have been employed for centuries.

Where the patch of open ground came close to the river, it funnelled into a narrow path between the river and the houses overlooking it. I placed two grenades in the weeds where only I would see them. If I could do so, I would lead Sean in this direction and explode them when he drew level.

I put more grenades at the base of two trees, knowing that I could not predict which direction the fight might go and duct-taped the three hastily made lightbulb petrol bombs to lampposts. This was highly illegal activity that would get me locked up and labelled as a terrorist if I got caught, but it is what you do when an evil wizard is coming for you.

My nerves were heightened by paranoia as I felt sure someone must be watching me. Each time a car went by I acted like I was doing nothing and a woman walking her spaniel caused me to stop for a solid five minutes while it ran around and took a poop on the grass.

Convinced I was going to get caught in the act, I came very close to wetting myself when Sean spoke. 'Good evening, Anastasia.' I jumped in fright, spinning about to face him. 'What are you doing there?'

His army of shilt were thankfully absent, contrary to Otto's predictions, but he had a new ogre with him, this one even bigger and nastier looking. The enormous, brutish beast towered over the wizard who was dressed in the same clothes as always, his cowl covering his head so all I could see of his face was his chin.

I wasted no time on words, drawing magical energy from my core to fire an orb at him. He didn't even flinch, the ogre's shield appearing in the nanosecond it took for my shot to get from me to them. I fired another, backing away in the hope they would follow me. Sean had all kinds of tricks to employ; I didn't know how many, but I saw a new one when the grass I was on flicked me into the air to sprawl at their feet.

'That was a simple earth spell,' he explained patiently. 'I could kill you without breaking sweat, Anastasia, but it would be a waste. I have need of your ability, as I have explained before. Stop this silliness and come with me before I grow bored and end your life.'

I looked up, staring into the depth of his cowl as I said, 'You're a killer.'

'Yes, I am. Taking your life wouldn't even register, I have killed so many. Yet I am not trying to kill you. I am offering you riches beyond those a mortal can perceive.' He stepped out from behind the ogre's shield, coming closer. Then he raised his voice. 'I grow bored of this senseless discussion, Anastasia. Come with me and do as I ask or die now.'

'I think we can find a third option.' The new voice joining the conversation belonged to Otto. I didn't need to look to know that the German accent I could hear was his. I scrambled backward on hands and feet, putting some distance between me and Sean.

Sean folded back the cowl of his coat to reveal his face for the first time. He was in his twenties, maybe not much older than me, and had blonde hair left to grow long so it would hang below his shoulders if he freed it from his man bun. A scar on the left side of his face pulled his upper lip so it was slightly misshapen, reminding me of my own scar.

'Where are the shilt?' asked Otto. 'If you propose to use them to attack the population in the hope that it will distract me, I'm afraid that will not work this time.'

Sean smiled, 'No, Otto. Nothing so callous. I have sent them to Bremen with a singular target. Just one woman and her family.'

'Heike,' Otto blurted. I glanced at Otto because he had stopped moving. Whatever Sean was telling him had caught the wizard by surprise and stalled his next move.

'Yes, Otto,' Sean laughed. 'If you hurry you might save them. Or you can stay here and fight me. The choice is yours.' Sean laughed again seeing the indecision on Otto's face. 'As long as you care, you will always be weaker than me, my German friend.'

A rage-filled roar filled the air as Otto unleashed a barrage of spells which sent a ripple across the ground just as lightning blasted down into it. Sean cackled as he parried and blocked each move. 'Tick tock, Otto. They may already be at her house.'

I had to duck and squint my eyes such was the intensity of the magic being unleashed. To people nearby, who must have rushed to their windows, it would have looked like a lightning storm taking place between the trees. I added my own blasts which remained as ineffective as ever, but I wasn't trying to hit Sean as much as I was trying to manoeuvre him. There were two grenades at the base of a tree just a few yards behind him and one of my lighter fluid bombs taped to a lamppost to his right. There was nothing magical about them and maybe that meant the ogre's shield wouldn't stop them.

Nothing Otto did got through; his sustained lightning attack created smoke in the clearing as Sean continued to laugh. The barrage of spells stopped as abruptly as they had started, an exhausted-looking Otto, heaving ragged breaths as hate shone from his eyes.

Sean still wasn't close enough for me to shoot at the grenades, but I had a bigger problem. I could tell Otto was about to abandon me so he could rescue whoever it was Sean threatened elsewhere. I shouted at him, 'No, Otto. I can't take him alone. He could be bluffing.'

But Otto slipped a glove onto his left hand, making motions with it as he glared unblinking at his enemy. A portal of shimmering air opened just behind him and as he stepped through it, he looked at me, his eyes filled with apology. 'I have to.'

My jaw dropped open as he disappeared. I couldn't believe it. I was alone and facing off against the ogre and his impenetrable shield plus Sean McGuire, the wizard not even Otto Schneider could beat. A moment ago, I had a little hope, now I had none. Unless …

When Sean spoke, it was with complete confidence. He looked serenely calm now that it was just me. 'You are correct, Anastasia, you cannot take me alone. Your little trick with source energy is fun but ultimately, it isn't designed to kill. Using it as a weapon is an ugly task it was never intended for.' I formed an orb in my right hand anyway. It wasn't all I had but they weren't to know that. Not yet, at least. Seeing the crackling ball of energy in my hand, he tilted his head to one side as a parent might to a misbehaving child. 'Shall we just dispense with all that? I have no intention of harming you. As I said before, I need you to do something for me. Something I cannot do for myself. You will be rewarded, or not, depending on whether you draw out this unnecessary need to resist.'

I moved a little to my left, Sean's eyes tracking me. 'Resist. That is an interesting choice of words. How old are you, Sean?' Looking around I could see that people had left their houses to see what caused all the light and noise. Their presence denied me the option of using the grenades, but as that plan failed, I perceived a new one.

I moved a little more to my left and backed up a few paces. This time Sean moved, stalking after me with the giant ogre by his side. Just a few more feet, that was all I needed. A few feet plus I had to stall him for a few more seconds because what I needed was just about to arrive.

'You wish to extend your life?' he asked. 'I am one hundred and sixty-four years old. If you come with me, you too will enjoy a prolonged lifespan.' I glanced to my left again. It was almost time, just a few more seconds.

I counted to three in my head, then threw an insult at the Irishman, 'Whatever it is you want me to do probably involves potatoes and dirt so I hope you'll forgive me when I say no thanks.' Then I launched my orb, but I shot high above his head to hit one of my home-made lighter fluid bombs. It ignited above his head, reigning liquid fire down so neither he nor the ogre could avoid it.

However, I didn't hang around to see what effect it had; I was running as fast as my prosthetic foot would let me go. A pizza delivery driver had been coming along the street, his constant glances at the house numbers convincing me he was about to make a stop. I had thrown the insult when he got off his bike, timing it so he would be at the door when I started my run and the furthest point from his bike.

A scream of rage followed me as I leapt down to street level, cursed the jolt of pain from my left stump and ran on regardless. I had to get Sean away from the populated area and I knew just the place. Little puffs of smoke from the bike's exhaust told me the engine was still running. It wasn't the most powerful machine, a two-fifty engine maybe, but it would take off like a scalded cat with my insignificant weight on it.

The pizza delivery man finished at the door, turning about to head back down the path but he wouldn't get to his bike before I did. At least, that was what I thought until he saw the crazy looking small person running directly for it. One moment, his eyes were wide inside his helmet, the next he was running, and he was going to get there the same time as me.

Then Sean let rip with a pulse of air. I didn't see it coming but I half expected it. That or flame, but as I heard the air rip through the trees on the avenue, I threw myself to the ground, rolled and came up just as it passed over me. The motorbike and the poor delivery driver caught the whole thing, the bike crashing over to its side and the delivery guy flying backward to land on his butt. I dived onto the bike, snatched it upright and gunned the throttle before I was even on it properly.

Lightning smashed into the spot where the bike had been just a heartbeat before, Sean deciding I would survive if he zapped me. The world went impossibly white for a second, the brightness of the lightning blinding me though I dared not slow down. When my vision returned less than a second later, I had travelled ten yards and was heading for a parked car.

As if my system could accept more adrenalin, I got a jolt of it along with the terror of an impending crash. I jammed my left foot into the ground as I leaned the bike and careened off the side of the car with a glancing blow.

Sean would catch me, I knew that much as I cranked the throttle and worked through the gearbox, the question was how soon. From where we were at the bottom of Shorts Way, I had a straight shot along the esplanade to the bridge at the bottom. There I would have to negotiate the busy junction, but busy often meant cars at a stand still and that might work in my favour. I was doing sixty miles per hour in four seconds and I wasn't throttling back no matter how scary it got.

Just then, I caught the surprised face of DS Spencer gawking at me from the driver's seat of his car as he went the other way. I didn't need to look behind me to know he was going to call it in and pursue me. Well, good luck. I've got an enraged wizard and his pet ogre on my arse, either of whom will happily kill you to get to me.

The bridge and the junction were right ahead, less than a hundred yards away and the gap around the queuing traffic was far too small to take at speed. I slowed, letting the throttle go rather than use the brakes and stood up on the pegs so I could see over the cars to judge whether I could time my approach and weave straight through. The place I wanted to go was on the other side of the rail track that crossed the river right next to the road bridge. It was empty industrial land which I saw on my way into the station two days ago.

There, I could use the last of my grenades without worrying I would kill anyone other than my targets and maybe myself. The bike had eaten up the last mile too fast for Sean to stop me but risking a glance behind me finally, there was no sign of him. He had to be pursuing, probably high above me though when I flicked a worried look to the night sky, there was no sign of him there either.

What I did see was flashing red and blue coming around the back of the castle and DS Spencer's face illuminated in his car as he sped along behind me beneath the streetlights. He slammed on his brakes as he got stuck behind the traffic, his unmarked car trying to force its way around through the oncoming traffic in the other lane but the road too tight to allow him passage. I zipped along the side of the cars, between them and the pavement where I had almost but not quite enough room, as I discovered when I started taking out door mirrors with the bike's handlebars. Horns blared behind me as I made it to the front, ignored the red light and got more horns as I shot in front of the cars feeding onto the bridge.

I was almost there, merging with the traffic coming off the bridge on the far side. All I had to do was find a way to pass under the elevated railway and I would make it to the wasteland on the other side.

All the way along the esplanade, my heart had beaten out of my chest as I expected Sean to blast the motorbike out from under me. It wasn't a wizard that got the bike, though, it was a double decker bus. You'd think I could have seen that coming, and I did, but it was too big to avoid. Even mashing the throttle as I came into the Rochester bound traffic leaving the bridge, it was still too wide for me to get out of its way and into the safety of the far lane. The human brain's ability to calculate time and distance told me I was about to get hit which softened the blow a little.

A little. But not much.

The bus caught the trailing edge of the rear wheel, only clipping it, but with enough force to kick the whole bike around. I opted to let go, the decision to do so made before the bus hit me, which probably saved my life, yet as I tumbled, the surgeon's stark warning to avoid blows to my head echoed in my ears once more. Would this be it? Crack my skull against the road, jolt the piece of shrapnel loose and save Sean the effort of killing me.

My arms came up to wrap around my head instinctively just before I hit the ground. My left foot caught the pavement first, the motion of the impact throwing me that way. I hit with enough force to jar the foot loose, the sensation of the cup being ripped from the stump one I recognised even as I continued to tumble. Out of control, it was my backpack that hit the ground next as screeching tyres and the sound of rending metal reached my ears.

Then, when my brain was telling me my skull was about to collide with the cruel tarmac, nothing happened. It was like I had been caught in a giant airbag as my spinning body decelerated under control until I was the right way up. Then my right foot touched down lightly on the pavement.

On the hump-backed bridge, the traffic flowing toward me had ceased to flow from what I could see, though horn sounds and crashes were still audible from beyond the central curved rise. Sean had chosen to save me, manipulating the air to form a cushion on which I would land. One might think it a generous gesture if his actions were not entirely self-motivated. He was on the opposite corner not far from Eddy's Tavern, gesturing to me to stop running. However, I could see the calm demeanour he had displayed before was gone. His long hair had caught fire and was mostly gone, burns to his scalp visible even from this distance.

With no time to lose and balancing on one leg, I gestured my surrender, which I hoped would buy me a few seconds of time as I hopped back to my left foot where it lay discarded in the road, the face of the driver in the nearest car a picture as I picked up my foot and shoved it back on. The boot I had been wearing was nowhere to be seen and I had no time to look for it. Another thing I didn't have was a bike; the rear wheel was neatly folded in two and the handlebars had snapped.

I couldn't make it to the waste land. Not by the route I intended anyway. I could only see one way of getting there now.

Sean waited patiently, no doubt convinced I would tire of running soon, but a shout changed all that as DS Spencer crossed through the traffic on the other side. He was on foot and very much out of breath as he wheezed in my direction. Worse yet, he wasn't alone. More police were coming as a squad car forced its way around the queue of cars. It would sweep around the mess I had made effectively cutting off any chance I had of escape.

Sean set it on fire.

I saw him move his hands and the next moment the interior of the squad car was on fire with the occupants still inside it. Screams preceded two flaming bodies rolling out of the car, the car itself crashing into the superstructure of the bridge where it stopped.

If I needed a spur to make me go for the crazy idea in my head, then that was it. Putting my head down, I swivelled on the spot, shoved off with my right foot and ran. Three steps later, I leapt into the air to get a foot on the railing that edged the bridge and then threw myself into the air.

Chapter 29

The railway bridge, a solid framework of iron, ran alongside the road bridge, but the gap between them was only a couple of yards wide. I didn't know if I could reach it, but gambled because I knew I would fall into the river below if I missed and perhaps I could escape that way. The flow would carry me downstream to open ground where I could fight without risking innocent casualties.

I was wrong, though, the river wasn't beneath me when I jumped. I was a couple of yards on from the edge of the river so if I missed, the only thing I would hit was the concrete twenty yards beneath me. I was out of sight from Sean too, so there would be no magical cushion of air to catch me this time either. Mercifully, my judgement was on the money and the distance was one a human could jump. I snagged the top edge of the bottom steel beam and let my body wrap around it.

My ribs hit the steel painfully but didn't drive the air from my chest. However, as I scrambled for purchase, trying to hook a knee on the lower flange to support myself, the ogre landed on the bridge right above my head. His feet were either side of my hands as he reached down to pluck me from the girder like a stuck kitten getting rescued.

Bystanders had to be gawping at me from the road bridge, the crash victims bailing out of their cars to watch the show and probably wondering who the enormous man was. As he reached for me, they cheered, the idiots thinking he was there to save me from falling.

I gave them something to look at when he lifted me to his eye level because I gave him a face full of energy blast. Believing I was beaten by my own foolishness, his shield wasn't in place to diffuse it, the full effect of it lifting him off his feet to an, 'Ahhh!' from the crowd behind as their collective gasps fused to make one noise.

He dropped me as he spun backwards, his body performing an almost perfect back flip as he somersaulted through the air. He crashed against the far side of the bridge and bounced off but my hope that he would stumble on the powerline and get fried didn't come to pass. Nor did he disintegrate as I expected him to.

Sean's voice rang out from somewhere above the iron structure. 'I told you, Anastasia. Your magic was made for peaceful, benign activities. You cannot kill with it. It only has that effect on the shilt because they are base creatures and the energy you wield believes them to be an abomination, which, essentially, they are.'

I ran, pulling my backpack around to my front as a train came toward me on the north-bound line. Rochester station was half a mile ahead, but that wasn't my destination. I needed to cross the rails and get to the wasteland on the other side and I wasn't going to do that with a train in the way. It might stop me from advancing but would also separate me from the ogre and that would do for now.

Sean continued to chat amiably, 'You have much to learn, Anastasia. I can teach you. It can be a partnership.'

'I just set your head on fire, Sean.' I shouted back. 'Shouldn't you be mad at me?' He was far too calm and in control of his emotions. I wanted him angry and irrational.

'There are bigger issues at stake, Anastasia. Greater consequences than death should I fail. My burns will heal.' While he prattled on, I took two grenades from my backpack. I couldn't see the ogre, but it had to be hiding in the structure on the other side of the bridge.

The sound of something scraping above my head told me I had that wrong just a second before it dropped down to land on top of me. While I was focused on the train and planning to strike when the tail end went by, the ogre had climbed over the top of the exposed steel frame.

I caught his shadow as it blocked out the light and had enough time to flatten myself but no more. The two grenades skittered away, the rest spilling from my backpack as the ogre grabbed the back of my hoody and hoisted me into the air. I pushed energy into my hand as I struggled, a fresh orb filling my hand though I had no target at which to throw it.

'Save yourself some pain,' called Sean loud enough for me to hear as the ogre threw me across the bridge. Terrified of hitting the electrified rail, there was nothing I could do to control my fall and I closed my eyes as I hit the tracks. How narrowly I missed, I would never know but the sensation of being fried from the inside didn't happen. Pain did. Lots and lots of pain as various parts of me reported colliding with things that were harder than me and my vision swam from the impact.

Struggling to see, something blocking out the moon gave me an aiming point even though I couldn't see properly. My automatic reaction to loose the orb of energy saved me from getting tossed around by the ogre again. This time he had the shield in place, but the light from my shot illuminated the area and showed me how close he was to the live rail. I couldn't hope to drive him back but maybe I could do better than that.

With no idea what effect it might have, my next shot went under his shield to hit the electrified rail. The pulse of raw energy connected with the huge source of electricity and exploded, arcs of my orb snaking out in all directions like lightning trying to escape the ground. I was lying between the tracks still, the gravel they use to backfill the tracks digging into my back painfully, but on the deck was the only safe place to be as the charge from the rail hit the ogre from behind and went to earth through him.

He staggered, the shield dropping as he took a step back. He wasn't going down, the giant creature tough enough to take that and stay on his feet. Tantalisingly, he wobbled, and I thought he was going to step on the live rail, but his foot passed over it, his strides wide enough to carry him to safety.

'Give up,' Sean's voice echoed off the steel structure.

'Not in my nature,' I growled to myself as I pushed myself off the rails. I was filthy, I was bleeding, my left foot hadn't gone back on properly and was threatening to come off again, but the ogre was stunned, and I saw exactly how to beat him. The grenades that spilled from my pack were on the rails to his rear. I was too close by far but with nothing to lose, I summoned magic through my body, pushing it out through my right hand to strike the grenades dead centre. I dropped my body as I let the blast go but the explosion caught me anyway. To my senses, it felt like the world ending.

The heat from it seared my skin and probably frazzled my hair. They were minor concerns because one thing it did do, was kill the ogre. His ruined body was thrown across the track again, the bulk of it creating a hazard for the next train as it came to rest on the northbound line. He was definitely dead this time, half his head missing along with both of his arms which was enough to convince me he wasn't going to walk it off.

Pushing my knuckles into the grit between the rails, I got to my knees and then to my feet, wriggling my left stump around painfully as I fought to get it to sit properly. 'Just you and me now, Sean!' I shouted into the darkness, readying another glowing orb.

It wasn't his voice that replied.

Despite all the noise from the road bridge a hundred yards away where emergency services were arriving to deal with the fire and crashed vehicles, a quiet, terrified voice reached my ears.

'Anastasia, I'm sorry.'

'Alex?'

Chapter 30

'He was in my apartment when I got home,' she cried, her voice echoing off the steel structure.

I closed my eyes and opened them again, my brain scrambling to find a new strategy that might allow me to win. I couldn't see one though, just as I couldn't see Alex even though I had heard her.

Into the darkness, I called, 'Where are you?'

Sean stepped out of the steelwork to show himself, his right hand up and open to show he had a conjuring ready to unleash. 'She is right here, Anastasia.' Two yards behind him, a pair of shilt dragged her into sight, emerging from between upright girders to stand on the southbound line. Sean spoke again to bring my attention back to his face. 'If you were not so unique, you would already be dead.' He indicated his head with his left hand. 'I will heal, but no one has injured me like this for a century and a half. I will make your life miserable, Anastasia Aaronson, and you will call me master. Now come to me or I will have them drain the life from her while you watch.'

As ultimatums go, his was a doozy.

'What now, soldier?' I asked myself, muttering the words quietly as I struggled to accept that I was defeated. There was no doubt in my mind that he would have Alex killed if I so much as suggested resistance on my part.

Acknowledging my no-win situation, I let the orb in my right hand go, the blue ball of energy receding into my hand as I lowered it. The last of my grenades were gone in a single wonderful explosion, but even if I had one left, I couldn't risk its use with Alex so close.

Sean still had his spell ready to fling and the shilt looked like they might devour Alex regardless of what I did, or Sean commanded. In that moment of hopelessness, I made the most reckless decision of my life: I accepted defeat.

'Ok, Sean. You win. I don't have the energy to fight any longer. I will do what you ask, just let my friend go, okay?'

He beckoned for me to walk to him. 'Your friend will be staying with us until you have retrieved that which I desire. If you comply, then I will allow her to go free.'

I expected as much. Which was why I shot her. I wouldn't claim I was certain I wasn't going to hurt her, but Sean drummed home the idea that my power wasn't intended for harm and I hadn't managed to kill him with it yet. The bigger danger, I felt, was her touching the live rail when she fell. Regardless, I went for it.

Sean didn't see it coming and neither did Alex. I had hidden my right hand in the pouch of my hoody as I formed an orb. Then, as I got within a foot of Sean, I drew it like I was a wild west gunslinger, the quickdraw too fast for Sean to stop. He thought I was going to fire it at him, but I was so close that I was able to slam into him like a rugby tackle. My arms went either side of his waist, my right hand free to fire the shot. Alex is such a big target (sorry, Alex), that I couldn't hope to miss.

The orb of fizzing energy struck her breastbone and tore her backwards from the shilts' grip. They got a half second to look surprised before I fired two more bolts at them. Diving at Sean had knocked him off balance but now it was a fight for survival as the shilt disintegrated and just Sean and I remained.

I knew he would be stronger than me, but he couldn't spell me at such close quarters and that made this my best tactic. He cried out in pain as I jabbed my left hand into him, its solidity ensuring my blows were more effective than my tiny muscles could achieve by themselves. A hard elbow came down on my neck, driving me to the ground as my left foot buckled under me, the stupid prosthetic betraying me where it still wasn't fitted properly. I staggered, going down to one knee as exhaustion, terror, breathlessness, and my injuries all demanded I stop for a rest.

I looked up to see the terrible grimace of his face as he swirled his right hand and the air in my lungs shut off again. It was one of the first spells he had ever used on me, and now it might be the last. I had so little fight left, and my body demanded oxygen I couldn't give it. Trying to gag, I saw the liquid seeping from his top. He was bleeding.

He was bleeding from exactly where I had been punching him with my left hand. My pulse hammered in my head, tiny dancing lights forming in my vision as I brought my left hand up and saw the ruined mess of it. The carbon fibre, ridiculously expensive prosthetic hand was broken, three of the fingers missing and the fourth forming a wicked spike.

I hadn't been punching his ribs, I had been stabbing him!

And I wasn't done yet. Not by half. I couldn't breathe, I was seconds from passing out, but I had enough left for one last roll of the dice. I think Sean saw it in my eyes, because his expression changed from triumphant to quizzical as I chose to stop dying and drove up off the ground with my right hand leading. He focused on that, which meant he didn't see my broken left hand as I thrust it into his chest.

I hit him somewhere just above his solar plexus, aiming for his heart and getting close enough. The air spell cutting off the supply of oxygen to my lungs was severed instantly, cool air from the river rushing into my lungs in great gasping breaths. Sean fell away from me, but the spike of my forefinger was lodged inside his chest, dragging me along and over to land on top of him.

Now it was his turn to gasp for breath as blood began to fill his lungs. He tried to lift his head just as I got a knee onto his rib cage and yanked my left hand free. It came away with a spray of blood and his head collapsed back to rest in the grime and litter between the rails.

'You think you've won?' he choked, blood coming from his mouth as he wheezed out the words. 'Humanity will soon be enslaved. Your one chance to escape that fate just slipped through your ignorant fingers.'

Angry to be listening to yet more cryptic shit, I grabbed his shirt with my right hand. 'What? What the hell are you talking about? Give me a straight answer.'

'Don't worry about it, Anastasia. You won't be around to see it.' His left hand shot out to grab the back of my head, pinning me in place as he lifted his head again and looked into my eyes, madness filling his. I saw too late as he struck out with his right arm, reaching for the live rail to electrocute us both. There was nothing I could do to stop him.

Chapter 31

'That really won't do,' said Alex calmly as she placed a foot on his right arm, pinning it in place three inches short of the electrified rail.

Seeing him defeated, I swung the spike of my left hand to impale the meaty part of his left bicep and kicked away from him as he screamed and let go of my head. A loud toot from a horn brought my eyes up from the ruined horror of his body to the train bearing down on us. We were on the southbound line and it was so close I could see the driver's terrified face.

Alex leapt over Sean, wrapped an arm around my torso and flung us both out of the way moments before the train ran straight over the fallen wizard. In the heartbeat before it took him, I swear I heard him shout something, but whatever it was, it was lost forever as the squeal of the screeching brakes drowned out all other sound.

Panting against me as she put me carefully back down on the ground, Alex said, 'This has not been my best evening ever.' I could not have agreed more. My left foot was missing again, but I didn't have the energy to stay upright anyway so I slumped down the side of the structure to rest against the cold steel.

Alex tapped my shoulder and pointed when she had my attention. 'Ana, what is that?'

I exhaled a hard breath staring at the enormous body still lying across the northbound line. 'Remember the really oversized man with all the other men who attacked us outside the cathedral?'

'Yes.'

'There you go.'

'Okay, but ... what is it? It's not human.'

The portion of his head that wasn't missing no longer had the enchantment to hide its true features apparently. 'I think it's an ogre. Shame really,' I smiled to myself, 'he was about the right size to date you.'

Alex gasped, 'Ooh, you cheeky mare.' But she laughed too, a tiny amount of dark humour in this awful environment.

'Can you see my foot?' I asked, unable to spot it. The train was still coming to a rest, but faces were gawking out of the windows at us. It covered the whole of the southbound track as far as I could see in either direction. If my foot was under it, I probably wasn't getting it back.

'Can I see your foot?' Alex repeated with a snigger. I don't know why, but it was funny; her laugh got me started and soon the people on the train were watching two insane women roaring as tears rolled down their cheeks.

'You know,' I managed despite my cackling, 'if this was *Die Hard*, the bad guy would be just about to reappear and try to kill us.'

I said it as a joke, but it was a sobering enough thought for us both to stop laughing and stare intently under the train. Shouts brought our attention away from the horrible concept. Swinging flashlights coming down the edge of the track from Rochester station heralding the police as they finally found their way to us.

How long had the fight lasted? One minute? Two? I felt more like a day had elapsed. When the police arrived, they stepped around the body of the ogre and the first to swing his flashlight on its face, became the first to swear in shock. He wasn't the last. It was indeed shocking, not just for its incredible size but also its obviously non-human features. The two small tusks protruding upward from the bottom jaw the biggest giveaway, but the piggish snout, slit eyes and strange pallor also received comment.

They were led by a uniformed sergeant who gave orders and relayed messages back to an incident unit already being established at Rochester station. While he did that, and fretted about the ogre, others made sure Alex and I were treated with care. They reassured us that we were safe now and would soon be evacuated from the area, but would have to go along the tracks to escape as there was no easy way off the bridge, or down from the elevated track; the station was the nearest exit point. When asked if I could walk, I pulled back the left leg of my jeans which drew a horrified squeal from the young male cop who asked the question.

Another cop found my missing foot, a middle-aged man with a beard, and he brought it over with an apologetic look. The train had sliced it in two, a small piece of the plastic still connecting the two parts but, like my left hand, it was completely unusable.

They could have waited for paramedics to bring a stretcher, but I wanted to go, and, as I may have mentioned, I don't exactly weigh a lot. Two cops linked hands to make a cradle on which I sat as they walked back to the station.

Inevitably, we were asked what had happened and how we ended up on the bridge. There hadn't been time to concoct a story and I had no idea what Alex would tell them about Sean grabbing her. Then there was the ogre which I couldn't possibly hope to explain.

Mercifully, it was hours before they got to question us properly, Alex and me straightening out our story with hushed whispers in the ambulance and the treatment room when no one was listening. I had been attacked for the umpteenth time as I left my apartment and stole the pizza delivery guy's motorbike to escape certain death. The desperate escape had been witnessed by DS Spencer who, I suspected, had been reluctant to corroborate his part in my statement. The man - no I have no idea who he was or why he was chasing me - chased me onto the bridge and cornered me there.

Alex had been on her way home via the pub at the end of the High Street right next to the bridge – Eddy's Tavern? – Yes, that's the one – when she saw me try to escape the man by jumping across to the rail bridge. She followed in the hope that she could help. She had already clobbered him once to stop him when he attacked me outside the library did you know?

We were asked about the body found on the northbound track, a large figure with strange features. We both lied that we had only seen him right at the end when the man chasing me fell under the train. 'Isn't he just a homeless man?' we both asked in our separate interviews.

My list of injuries was extensive, though incredibly nothing was broken. Unless you count my prosthetic hand and foot, of course. I got stitches, painkillers, and dressings and they left me to sleep. A trauma counsellor was at hand if I wanted to talk. Alex came to find me, her clothes like mine had been discarded as unsalvageable, so she wore a hospital gown and complained that her bum kept sticking out of the gap at the back.

In the morning, she would be discharged, and Abi had already agreed to go by her place to pick up some clothes. I spoke with Professor Grayhawk to yet again tell him I wouldn't be in work the next day. Of course, he told me to take all the time I needed and to only return when I felt up to it. I would be there tomorrow if I could, the quiet and normality of it something I craved deeply. I couldn't go anywhere though. Among my list of ailments was a ruptured kidney. The diagnosis explained why it hurt so much more than I thought some bruising ought to. It would keep me in for a few days they said, which was okay because it would take that long to make me a new hand. The Real Limb people had been contacted and would get right on with making one. The foot would be easier to come by.

As I drifted off to sleep that night, one question battled against my fatigue: Where was Otto?

Chapter 32

Sean hadn't bluffed about sending the shilt to Bremen; he sent them in force. Without Otto there, the city was essentially unguarded against supernatural attack and the shilt were only too happy to provide it. Like most others in the immortal realm, they felt they had a score to settle with Otto Schneider; he had killed countless thousands of their kind.

Had Heike Dressler been at home that evening, she, her husband, and their children would have been killed as more than a hundred shilt came to feast on their life energy. But the shilt found an empty house, the Dresslers taking a well-earned break in Greece where, at the time the shilt were breaking into their house, they were enjoying a meze platter in a taverna near their hotel.

The alarm at the house drew the local police who arrived to find Otto Schneider dispatching any shilt who were not quick enough to escape.

By the time he returned to Rochester the fight was finished and when he saw Anastasia being carried out of the station to an Ambulance, he left, content that she was safe. A short while later, the commissioner emerged once more from the elevator onto the top floor of the Alliance's secret underground bunker in London.

'I understand from observers on the ground in Rochester that we almost lost her.' The commissioner was trying to make a point. He still felt the woman should be brought in and debriefed. He was close to doing it too, only his superior's instruction to work with the wizard holding him back.

Otto inclined his head, neither arguing nor agreeing. 'I can only tell you that she is still alive and is most likely stronger for the conflict she survived.'

'She would be safer inside this bunker where we can protect her and train her. Here, we could find out what she can do and how we might employ her assets.'

Otto was growing tired of the discussion but tried to make the point one last time in a calm tone. 'What is the demons' interest in her?'

Swinton frowned at the question. 'I don't know. Surely, that is why we need to bring her in.' He felt he had the winning point.

Otto pinched his nose with thumb and forefinger. 'I can assure you she has no idea what they want her for. She doesn't even know demons exist yet. We need to leave her out there so they will play their hand. Only then will we know why she is of such interest. It has to be something big and we have to find out what their aim is before the demons can achieve it.'

'So we just leave her at their mercy?'

'That is my recommendation. Watch. Record. Report. But if we intervene too soon, we may never know what they wanted her for.'

Swinton argued, 'What if they kill her? What do we gain then? What if they take her to the immortal realm?'

Otto decided enough was enough. He believed the commissioner would obey his superior's orders. That they matched Otto's was a happy coincidence. Walking to the elevator to ride it to the surface, he replied to the commissioner's banal questions. 'If they wanted her dead, she would be. If they take her to the immortal realm, I will go there and get her back.' He paused as a thought occurred to him. 'One thing your men can do ...'

'Go on,' replied the commissioner thinking it typical of the German to demand something immediately after rudely walking away.

'Get me an item of her clothing.'

As the elevator doors closed, the commissioner's voice faded and was only just audible. 'An item of her clothing? Whatever for?'

Epilogue: Daniel's Chagrin

'How many familiars have you lost this year, Daniel?' It was a rhetorical question, but Beelzebub expected an answer anyway.

Reluctantly, and annoyed that his plans had arrived at this result, Daniel said, 'Three. My Lord the issue throughout has been Otto Schneider.'

Beelzebub held up a finger to silence his underling. 'The issue has been your ambition, Daniel. I do not condemn you for it, but I expect to profit by it. Your ambition has always outweighed your ability. That is why you have remained in the position your currently occupy. Nathaniel will remain your overseer and you should be thankful I have tolerated your devious subterfuge for this long.'

'My Lord, it is only my wish to serve our kind.'

Again, Beelzebub cut him off. 'Were that so, Daniel, you and I would not be having this conversation. I suspect that you are plotting something. So, be warned; if I discover that you are keeping things from me that I ought to know, or in any way deliberately undermining Nathaniel, I will treat you as a traitor and when we return to earth as mortals, I will kill you.'

Obediently, Daniel said, 'Yes, my Lord,'

'The humans are gaining power. The number of them developing the ability to channel ley line energy or shift forms is unexpected. I believe they will attempt to resist us.' Daniel remained quiet while Beelzebub looked into the distance and contemplated what the resurgence of human magic might mean. 'We will crush them nevertheless; they have no ability to comprehend the power and might I have in reserve for them.'

Daniel had been waiting for Beelzebub to reveal that he already knew of the woman with the extraordinary power; the one who could summon source energy. It wasn't in his nature to hold his breath, but he came close to it nevertheless when the ruler of all demons started talking about the humans growing stronger. It was true; finding familiars of worth had been difficult a century ago, and almost impossible a century before that. Now though, he could reliably find at least one good one in most major cities. Often, they had no idea of their power, or were suppressing it because they didn't want to explore it. The good news was that he might still be the only one who knew about Anastasia Aaronson.

Beelzebub sniffed, drawing air through his nose as he often did before he gave an order. 'You will find Nathaniel a new familiar, Daniel. A good one. You will do that before you furnish your own needs. When I gave you Sean McGuire, it was so that you could capture Otto Schneider and stop his interfering. You failed to do that and lost a good asset. How was Sean McGuire killed?' the ruler asked as if the question had just occurred to him.

'It must be the work of Otto Schneider, my Lord. The immortal wizard sought revenge and I believe he now has it. The shilt were killed at the same time, and, I believe, an ogre he employed to lead them.'

Beelzebub nodded. 'Very well. With so many familiars lost, I will be sending others to do the work you have made your own for the last few hundred years. Restock us, Daniel. Do that and do it well and I may overlook some of your other indiscretions.'

Beelzebub walked away without another word, leaving Daniel to silently fume and consider his next move. The woman was the key to it all. Her power combined with her mortality would give him access to the artefact in Rochester. He knew there were other artefacts out there, but he had poured significant resource into locating the one that he wanted. He knew where several others were, but the important one, the one which would make him rise above his peers was buried under the cathedral, he believed. This time he was going to have to go himself. The stakes were too high now and Beelzebub wasn't the only one watching him. He would play the role of obedient servant for a short while, just until another issue diverted their attention and he would use the time to recruit allies.

Then he would do what he should have done in the first place and take Anastasia Aaronson himself.

The End

Author Note:

H ello,

Its nearly midnight in my house as I sit on the couch writing this short note. I have a snoring dachshund next to me and two more on another couch adjacent to this one. My wife and child are upstairs also sleeping.

I guess I'm the dumb one.

This book was harder to write than any book since probably the very first one. That one took me five years because I had no idea what I was doing at the time. The reason this one was so hard was because the concept for it came from a short story I wrote, and I wrote the short story because I felt the Anastasia book I had already written needed a small prequel. That book was **Demon Bound** which now makes much more sense as the second book in her series. I'll be ploughing into her third adventure shortly but writing the second story first and then deciding I needed to write a full novel to lead into it, required some ingenuity and took as long to write as the previous three books.

I am still being asked how long this series will be, and the answer is still that I don't know. I have a clear idea about what I want to write, but my brain keeps seeing new possibilities which is how two series, one about a detective wizard and one about an injured solider who develops supernatural abilities, ended up both being the same series. One thing I can say for sure is that I will keep on writing. It is just too much fun to ever consider stopping.

For reference, if you are picking this book up years after I wrote it, the Corona Virus is sweeping the planet, turning everyone nuts as theme parks which have never closed, close for the first time, sporting events are cancelled and international flight looks set to be grounded soon. It is a scary time because people will lose loved ones that would not otherwise have died. I've no wish to dwell on that, I am just using it as an historic marker.

You will have seen in the dedication that I have a baby coming. At the time of publication, my daughter, the only one I ever expect to get, will be just a few weeks from being due to arrive. That prospect makes me very happy, not just because of how much my wife will smile, but because life is a rollercoaster if you want it to be.

I think that's probably enough rambling for now. It's late, and the celebratory rum and coke I poured when I typed 'The End' hit my bloodstream already. Anastasia requires me to get back to the words, so until next time, take care.

Steve Higgs

More Books By Steve Higgs

Blue Moon Investigations
Paranormal Nonsense
The Phantom of Barker Mill
Amanda Harper Paranormal Detective
The Klowns of Kent
Dead Pirates of Cawsand
In the Doodoo With Voodoo
The Witches of East Malling
Crop Circles, Cows and Crazy Aliens
Whispers in the Rigging
Bloodlust Blonde – a short story
Paws of the Yeti
Under a Blue Moon – A Paranormal
Detective Origin Story
Night Work
Lord Hale's Monster
The Herne Bay Howlers
Undead Incorporated
The Ghoul of Christmas Past
The Sandman
Jailhouse Golem
Shadow in the Mine
Ghost Writer

Felicity Philips Investigates
To Love and to Perish
Tying the Noose
Aisle Kill Him
A Dress to Die For
Wedding Ceremony Woes

Patricia Fisher Cruise Mysteries
The Missing Sapphire of Zangrabar
The Kidnapped Bride
The Director's Cut
The Couple in Cabin 2124
Doctor Death
Murder on the Dancefloor
Mission for the Maharaja
A Sleuth and her Dachshund in Athens
The Maltese Parrot
No Place Like Home

Patricia Fisher Mystery Adventures
What Sam Knew
Solstice Goat
Recipe for Murder
A Banshee and a Bookshop
Diamonds, Dinner Jackets, and Death
Frozen Vengeance
Mug Shot
The Godmother
Murder is an Artform
Wonderful Weddings and Deadly
Divorces
Dangerous Creatures

Patricia Fisher: Ship's Detective Series
The Ship's Detective
Fitness Can Kill
Death by Pirates
First Dig Two Graves

Albert Smith Culinary Capers
Pork Pie Pandemonium
Bakewell Tart Bludgeoning
Stilton Slaughter
Bedfordshire Clanger Calamity
Death of a Yorkshire Pudding
Cumberland Sausage Shocker
Arbroath Smokie Slaying
Dundee Cake Dispatch
Lancashire Hotpot Peril
Blackpool Rock Bloodshed
Kent Coast Oyster Obliteration
Eton Mess Massacre
Cornish Pasty Conspiracy

Realm of False Gods
Untethered magic
Unleashed Magic
Early Shift
Damaged but Powerful
Demon Bound
Familiar Territory
The Armour of God
Live and Die by Magic
Terrible Secrets

About the Author

At school, the author was mostly disinterested in every subject except creative writing, for which, at age ten, he won his first award. However, calling it his first award suggests that there have been more, which there have not. Accolades may come but, in the meantime, he is having a ball writing mystery stories and crime thrillers and claims to have more than a hundred books forming an unruly queue in his head as they clamour to get out. He lives in the south-east corner of England with a duo of lazy sausage dogs. Surrounded by rolling hills, brooding castles, and vineyards, he doubts he will ever leave, the beer is just too good.

If you are a social media fan, you should copy the link below into your browser to join my very active Facebook group. You'll find a host of friends waiting there, some of whom have been with me from the very start.

My Facebook group get first notification when I publish anything new, plus cover reveals and free short stories, but more than that, they all interact with each other, sharing inside jokes, and answering question.

 facebook.com/stevehiggsauthor

You can also keep updated with my books via my website:

g https://stevehiggsbooks.com/

Printed in Great Britain
by Amazon

38533526R00108